OROONOKO

OROONOKO

DOVER THRIFT EDITIONS

Aphra Behn

DOVER PUBLICATIONS, INC.
MINEOLA, NEW YORK

DOVER THRIFT EDITIONS

General Editor: Susan L. Rattiner

Editor of This Volume: Jim Miller

Bibliographical Note

This Dover edition, first published in 2017, is an unabridged republication of *Oroonoko: or, the Royal Slave*, originally published in 1688 by William Canning, London. A new introductory Note has been specially prepared for this edition.

International Standard Book Number

ISBN-13: 978-0-486-81483-4
ISBN-10: 0-486-81483-1

Manufactured in the United States by LSC Communications
81483101   2017
www.doverpublications.com

Note

Aphra Behn, playwright, poet, and writer of prose fiction, was born in England around 1640. The exact date and location of her birth and even her original name are unknown, and the information regarding her early life is scant and unreliable. What is known is that she was one of the first English women to earn a living through her writing alone, and that she enjoyed both fame and notoriety during her lifetime. It is believed that she served Charles II and his Restoration court as a spy in Antwerp in 1666 during the Second Anglo-Dutch War, and that soon after her return to London she adopted "Aphra Behn" as her professional name and began writing for the stage. She soon found success with both dramas and comedies, and became an accepted part of the London literary scene. In all, Behn would write nineteen plays, and upon her death on April 16, 1689, she was buried in Westminster Abbey—a great honor indeed for a woman writer of the time.

Aphra Behn is probably best remembered today not for her plays, but for *Oroonoko*. This short work was published in 1688 and it concerns an enslaved African prince who is sold to British colonists in Suriname. There he meets the narrator of the story and the plot soon unfolds with unexpected results. *Oroonoko* was published less than a year before Behn died, and is notable for its treatment and exploration of gender, race, and slavery. It is also considered an important text in the development of the novel in its modern form.

OROONOKO

To The Right Honourable The Lord Maitland.

My Lord, since the world is grown so nice and critical upon dedications, and will needs be judging the book by the wit of the patron, we ought with a great deal of circumspection, to choose a person against whom there can be no exception, and whose wit and worth truly merits all that one is capable of saying upon that occasion.

The most part of dedications are charged with flattery, and if the world knows a man has some vices, they will not allow one to speak of his virtues. This, my Lord, is for want of thinking rightly; if men would consider with reason, they would have another sort of opinion and esteem of dedications and would believe almost every great man has enough to make him worthy of all that can be said of him there. My Lord, a picture drawer, when he intends to make a good picture, essays the face many ways, and in many lights, before he begins, that he may choose from the several turns of it which is most agreeable and gives it the best grace; and if there be a scar, an ungrateful mole, or any little defect, they leave it out; and yet make the picture extremely like. But he who has the good fortune to draw a face that is exactly charming in all its parts and features, what colours or agreements can be added to make it finer? All that he can give is but its due; and glories in a piece whose original alone gives it its perfection. An ill hand may diminish, but a good hand cannot augment its beauty. A poet is a painter in his way; he draws to the life, but in another kind; we draw the nobler part, the soul and mind; the pictures of the pen shall outlast those of the pencil, and even worlds themselves. 'Tis a short chronicle of those lives that possibly would be forgotten by other historians, or lie neglected there, however deserving an immortal fame; for men of eminent parts are as exemplary as even monarchs themselves: and virtue is a noble lesson to be learned, and 'tis by comparison we can judge and choose. 'Tis by such illustrious precedents as your Lordship the world can be bettered and refined; when a great part of the lazy nobility shall with shame behold the admirable accomplishments of a man so great and so young.

Your Lordship has read innumerable volumes of men and books, not vainly for the gust of novelty, but knowledge, excellent knowledge: like the industrious bee, from every flower you return laden with the precious dew, which you are sure to turn to the public good. You hoard no one perfection, but lay it all out in the glorious service of your religion and country; to both which you are a useful and necessary honour: they both want such supporters, and 'tis only men of so elevated parts and fine knowledge, such noble principles of loyalty and religion this nation sighs for. Where shall we find a man so young, like Saint Augustine, in the midst of all his youth and gaiety, teaching the world divine precepts, true notions of faith, and excellent morality, and, at the same time, be also a perfect pattern of all that accomplish a great man? You have, my Lord, all that refined wit that charms, and the affability that obliges; a generosity that gives a lustre to your nobility; that hospitality and greatness of mind that engages the world and that admirable conduct that so well instructs it. Our nation ought to regret and bemoan their misfortunes, for not being able to claim the honour of the birth of a man who is so fit to serve His Majesty and his kingdoms in all great and public affairs, and to the glory of your nation be it spoken, it produces more considerable men, for all fine sense, wit, wisdom, breeding, and generosity (for the generality of the nobility) than all other nations can boast; and the fruitfulness of your virtues sufficiently make amends for the barrenness of your soil: which, however, cannot be incommode to your Lordship, since your quality and the veneration that the commonalty naturally pay their lords creates a flowing plenty there—that makes you happy. And to complete your happiness, my Lord, Heaven has blessed you with a lady, to whom it has given all the graces, beauties, and virtues of her sex; all the youth, sweetness of nature, of a most illustrious family, and who is a most rare example to all wives of quality for her eminent piety, easiness, and condescension: and as absolutely merits respect from all the world, as she does that passion and resignation she receives from your Lordship: and which is, on her part, with so much tenderness returned. Methinks your tranquil lives are an image of the new made and beautiful pair in paradise: and 'tis the prayers and wishes of all, who have the honour to know you, that it may eternally so continue with additions of all the blessings this world can give you.

My Lord, the obligations I have to some of the great men of your nation, particularly to your Lordship, gives me an ambition of making my acknowledgements, by all the opportunities I can; and such humble fruits as my industry produces I lay at your Lordship's feet. This is a true story of a man gallant enough to merit your protection; and, had he always been so fortunate, he had not made so inglorious an end: the royal slave I had the honour to know in my travels to the other world; and though I had none above me in that country, yet I wanted power to preserve this great man. If there be anything that seems Romantic, I beseech your Lordship to consider these countries do, in all things, so far differ from ours, that they produce unconceivable wonders; at least they appear so to us because new and strange. What I have mentioned I have taken care should be truth, let the critical reader judge as he pleases. 'Twill be no commendation to the book to assure your Lordship I writ it in a few hours, though it may serve to excuse some of its faults of connection, for I never rested my pen a moment for thought: 'tis purely the merit of my slave that must render it worthy of the honour it begs; and the author of that of subscribing herself,

My Lord,
your Lordship's most obliged
and obedient servant
A. Behn.

THE HISTORY OF THE ROYAL SLAVE

I DO not pretend, in giving you the history of this royal slave, to entertain my reader with the adventures of a feigned hero, whose life and fortunes fancy may manage at the poet's pleasure; nor in relating the truth, design to adorn it with any accidents, but such as arrived in earnest to him: and it shall come simply into the world, recommended by its own proper merits and natural intrigues, there being enough of reality to support it, and to render it diverting, without the addition of invention.

I was myself an eye-witness to a great part of what you will find here set down, and what I could not be witness of I received from the mouth of the chief actor in this history, the hero himself, who gave us the whole transactions of his youth, and though I shall omit, for brevity's sake, a thousand little accidents of his life, which, however pleasant to us, where history was scarce, and adventures very rare, yet might prove tedious and heavy to my reader in a world where he finds diversions for every minute new and strange. But we who were perfectly charmed with the character of this great man were curious to gather every circumstance of his life.

The scene of the last part of his adventures lies in a colony in America called Surinam in the West Indies. But before I give you the story of this gallant slave, 'tis fit I tell you the manner of bringing them to these new colonies; for those they make use of there are not natives of the place, for those we live with in perfect amity, without daring to command 'em, but on the contrary, caress 'em with all the brotherly and friendly affection in the world; trading with 'em for their fish, venison, buffaloes' skins and little rarities, as marmosets, a sort of monkey as big as a rat or weasel, but of a marvellous and delicate shape, and has face and hands like an human creature, and cousheries, a little beast in the form and fashion of a lion, as big as a kitten, but so exactly made in all parts like that noble beast that it is it in miniature. Then for little parakeetoes, great parrots, macaws, and a thousand other birds and beasts of wonderful and surprising forms, shapes, and colours, for skins of prodigious snakes, of which there are some threescore yards in length, as is the skin of one that may be seen at His Majesty's anti-quary's, where are also some rare flies, of amazing forms and co-lours, presented to 'em by myself, some as big as my fist, some less, and all of various excellencies, such as art cannot imitate. Then we trade for feathers, which they order into all shapes, make themselves little short habits of 'em, and glorious wreaths for their heads, necks, arms, and legs, whose tinctures are unconceivable. I had a set of these presented to me, and I gave 'em to the King's theatre, and it was the dress of the Indian Queen, infinitely admired by persons of quality, and were unimitable. Besides these, a thousand little knacks and rarities in nature, and some of art, as their baskets, weapons, aprons, etc. We dealt with 'em with beads of all colours, knives, axes, pins, and needles, which they used only as tools to drill holes with in their ears, noses, and lips, where they hang a great many little things, as long beads, bits of tin, brass, or silver, beat thin, and any shiny trinket. The beads they weave into aprons about a quarter of an ell long, and of the same breadth, working them very prettily in flowers of several colours of beads, which apron they wear just before 'em, as Adam and Eve did the fig leaves; the men wearing a long strip of linen, which they deal with us for. They thread these beads also on long cotton threads, and make girdles to tie their aprons to, which come twenty times or more about the waist and then cross, like a shoulder belt, both ways and round their necks, arms and legs. This adornment, with their long black hair and the face painted in little specks or flowers here and there, makes 'em a wonderful figure to behold. Some of the beauties, which indeed are finely shaped, as almost all are, and who have pretty features, are very charming and novel, for they have all that is called beauty, except the colour, which is a reddish yellow or, after a new oiling, which they often use to themselves, they are of the colour of a new brick, but smooth, soft, and sleek.

They are extreme modest and bashful, very shy, and nice of being touched. And though they are all thus naked, if one lives forever among 'em, there is not to be seen an indecent action, or glance, and being continually used to see one another unadorned, so like our first parents before the Fall, it seems as if they had no wishes, there being nothing to heighten curiosity, but all you can see, you see at once, and every moment see; and where there is no novelty, there can be no curiosity. Not but I have seen a handsome young Indian dying for love of a very beautiful young Indian maid; but all his courtship was to fold his arms, pursue her with his eyes, and sighs were all his language, while she, as if no such lover were present, or rather, as if she desired none such, carefully guarded her eyes from beholding him, and never approached him, but she looked down with all the blushing modesty I have seen in the most severe and cautious of our world. And these people represented to me an absolute idea of the first state of innocence, before Man knew how to sin, and 'tis most evident and plain that simple Nature is the most harmless, inoffensive, and virtuous mistress. 'Tis she alone, if she were permitted, that better instructs the world than all the inventions of Man. Religion would here but destroy that tranquillity they possess by ignorance, and laws would but teach 'em to know offence, of which now they have no notion. They once made mourning and fasting for the death of the English governor, who had given his hand to come on such a day to 'em, and neither came, nor sent; believing, when once a man's word was passed, nothing but death could or should prevent his keeping it, and when they saw he was not dead, they asked him what name they had for a man who promised a thing he did not do. The governor told them such a man was a liar, which was a word of infamy to a gentleman. Then one of 'em replied, "Governor, you are a liar and guilty of that infamy." They have a native justice which knows no fraud, and they understand no vice, or cunning, but when they are taught by the white men. They have plurality of wives, which, when they grow old, they serve those that succeed 'em, who are young, but with a servitude easy and respected, and unless they take slaves in war, they have no other attendants.

Those on that continent where I was had no king, but the oldest war captain was obeyed with great resignation. A war captain is a man who has led them on to battle with conduct and success, of whom I shall have occasion to speak more hereafter, and of some other of their customs and manners as they fall in my way.

With these people, as I said, we live in perfect tranquillity and good understanding, as it behoves us to do, they knowing all the places where to seek the best food of the country and the means of getting it; and for very small and unvaluable trifles, supply us with what 'tis impossible for us to get, for they do not only in the wood and over the savannahs in hunting supply the parts of hounds by swiftly scouring through those almost impassable places, and by the mere activity of their feet, run down the nimblest deer, and other eatable beasts, but in the water one would think they were gods of the rivers, or fellow citizens of the deep, so rare an art they have in swimming, diving, and almost living in water, by which they command the less swift inhabitants of the floods. And then for shooting, what they cannot take or reach with their hands, they do with arrows, and have so admirable an aim, that they will split almost an hair, and at any distance that an arrow can reach they will shoot down oranges and other fruit, and only touch the stalk with the darts' points that they may not hurt the fruit. So that they being on all occasions very useful to us, we find it absolutely necessary to caress 'em as friends and not to treat 'em as slaves; nor dare we do other, their numbers so far surpassing ours in that continent. Those then whom we make use of to work in our plantations of sugar are negroes, black slaves altogether, which are transported thither in this manner.

Those who want slaves make a bargain with a master, or captain of a ship and contract to pay him so much a piece, a matter of twenty pound a head for as many as he agrees for and to pay for 'em when they shall be delivered on such a plantation. So that when there arrives a ship laden with slaves, they who have so contracted go aboard and receive their number by lot; and perhaps in one lot that may be for ten, there may happen to be three or four men, the rest, women and children. Or, be there more or less of either sex, you are obliged to be contented with your lot.

Coramantien, a country of blacks so called, was one of those places in which they found the most advantageous trading for these slaves, and thither most of our great traders in that merchandise trafficked, for that nation is very warlike and brave and, having a continual campaign, being always in hostility with one neighbouring prince or other, they had the fortune to take a great many captives, for all they took in battle were sold as slaves; at least, those common men who could not ransom themselves. Of these slaves so taken, the general only has all the profit and of these generals, our captains and masters of ships buy all their freights.

The king of Coromantien was himself a man of a hundred and odd years old, and had no son, though he had many beautiful black wives; for most certainly there are beauties that can charm of that colour. In his younger years he had had many gallant men to his sons, thirteen of which died in battle, conquering when they fell, and he had only left him for his successor one grandchild, son to one of these dead victors, who, as soon as he could bear a bow in his hand, and a quiver at his back, was sent into the field to be trained up by one of the oldest generals to war, where from his natural inclination to arms, and the occasions given him with the good conduct of the old general, he became, at the age of seventeen, one of the most expert captains and bravest soldiers that ever saw the field of Mars. So that he was adored as the wonder of all that world, and the darling of the soldiers. Besides, he was adorned with a native beauty so transcending all those of his gloomy race, that he struck an awe and reverence even in those that knew not his quality, as he did in me, who beheld him with surprise and wonder when afterwards he arrived in our world.

He had scarce arrived at his seventeenth year when fighting by his side the general was killed with an arrow in his eye, which the Prince Oroonoko (for so was this gallant Moor called) very narrowly avoided; nor had he, if the general, who saw the arrow shot, and perceiving it aimed at the prince, had not bowed his head between, on purpose to receive it in his own body rather than it should touch that of the prince, and so saved him. 'Twas then, afflicted as Oroonoko was, that he was proclaimed general in the old man's place, and then it was, at the finishing of that war, which had continued for two years, that the prince came to court, where he had hardly been a month together, from the time of his fifth year to that of seventeen; and 'twas amazing to imagine where it was he learned so much humanity; or, to give his accomplishments a juster name, where 'twas he got that real greatness of soul, those refined notions of true honour, that absolute generosity, and that softness that was capable of the highest passions of love and gallantry, whose objects were almost continually fighting men, or those mangled, or dead, who heard no sounds but those of war and groans. Some part of it we may attribute to the care of a French man of wit and learning, who finding it turn to very good account to be a sort of royal tutor to this young black, and perceiving him very ready, apt, and quick of apprehension, took a great pleasure to teach him morals, language, and science, and was for it extremely beloved and valued by him. Another reason was he loved when he came from war to see all the English gentlemen that traded thither, and did not only learn their language, but that of the Spaniards also, with whom he traded afterwards for slaves.

I have often seen and conversed with this great man, and been a witness to many of his mighty actions, and do assure my reader, the most illustrious courts could not have produced a braver man, both for greatness of courage and mind, a judgement more solid, a wit more quick, and a conversation more sweet and diverting. He knew almost as much as if he had read much; he had heard of and admired the Romans, he had heard of the late Civil Wars in England and the deplorable death of our great monarch, and would discourse of it with all the sense, and abhorrence of the injustice imaginable. He had an extreme good and graceful mien, and all the civility of a well-bred great man. He had nothing of barbarity in his nature, but in all points addressed himself as if his education had been in some European court.

This great and just character of Oroonoko gave me an extreme curiosity to see him, especially when I knew he spoke French and English and that I could talk with him. But though I had heard so much of him, I was as greatly surprised when I saw him as if I had heard nothing of him; so beyond all report I found him. He came into the room and addressed himself to me and some other women with the best grace in the world. He was pretty tall, but of a shape the most exact that can be fancied. The most famous statuary could not form the figure of a man more admirably turned from head to foot. His face was not of that brown, rusty black which most of that nation are, but a perfect ebony, or polished jet. His eyes were the most aweful that could be seen and very piercing, the white of 'em being like snow, as were his teeth. His nose was rising and Roman, instead of African and flat. His mouth, the finest shaped that could be seen, far from those great turned lips, which are so natural to the rest of the Negroes. The whole proportion and air of his face was so noble and exactly formed that, bating his colour, there could be nothing in nature more beautiful, agreeable, and handsome. There was no one grace wanting that bears the standard of true beauty. His hair came down to his shoulders, by the aids of art, which was by pulling it out with a quill and keeping it combed, of which he took particular care. Nor did the perfections of his mind come short of those of his person, for his discourse was admirable upon almost any subject, and whoever had heard him speak would have been convinced of their errors, that all fine wit is confined to the white men, especially to those of Christendom, and would have confessed that Oroonoko was as capable even of reigning well and of governing as wisely, had as great a soul, as politic maxims, and was as sensible of power, as any prince civilized in the most refined schools of humanity and learning, or the most illustrious courts.

This prince, such as I have described him, whose soul and body were so admirably adorned, was (while yet he was in the court of his grandfather), as I said, as capable of love as 'twas possible for a brave and gallant man to be; and in saying that, I have named the highest degree of love, for sure, great souls are most capable of that passion. I have already said, the old general was killed by the shot of an arrow, by the side of this prince in battle, and that Oroonoko was made general. This old dead hero had one only daughter left of his race: a beauty that to describe her truly one need say only she was female to the noble male, the beautiful black Venus to our young Mars, as charming in her person as he and of delicate virtues. I have seen an hundred white men sighing after her and making a thousand vows at her feet, all vain and unsuccessful. And she was indeed too great for any but a prince of her own nation to adore.

Oroonoko, coming from the wars, which were now ended, after he had made his court to his grandfather, he thought in honour he ought to make a visit to Imoinda, the daughter of his foster father, the dead general, and to make some excuses to her, because his preservation was the occasion of her father's death, and to present her with those slaves that had been taken in this last battle, as the trophies of her father's victories. When he came, attended by all the young soldiers of any merit, he was infinitely surprised at the beauty of this fair queen of night, whose face and person was so exceeding all he had ever beheld, that lovely modesty with which she received him, that softness in her look and sighs upon the melancholy occasion of this honour that was done by so great a man as Oroonoko, and a prince of whom she had heard such admirable things, the awefulness wherewith she received him, and the sweetness of her words and behaviour while he stayed, gained a perfect conquest over his fierce heart and made him feel the victor could be subdued. So that having made his first compliments, and presented her an hundred and fifty slaves in fetters, he told her with his eyes that he was not insensible of her charms; while Imoinda, who wished for nothing more than so glorious a conquest, was pleased to believe she understood that silent language of new-born love, and from that moment put on all her additions to beauty.

The prince returned to court with quite another humour than before; and though he did not speak much of the fair Imoinda, he had the pleasure to hear all his followers speak of nothing but the charms of that maid, insomuch that, even in the presence of the old king, they were extolling her and heightening, if possible, the beauties they had found in her. So that nothing else was talked of, no other sound was heard in every corner where there were whisperers, but "Imoinda! Imoinda!."

'Twill be imagined Oroonoko stayed not long before he made his second visit, nor, considering his quality, not much longer before he told her he adored her. I have often heard him say that he admired by what strange inspiration he came to talk things so soft, and so passionate, who never knew love, nor was used to the conversation of women, but (to use his own words) he said, most happily, some new, until then unknown power instructed his heart and tongue in the language of love and at the same time in favour of him inspired Imoinda with a sense of his passion. She was touched with what he said and returned it all in such answers as went to his very heart, with a pleasure unknown before. Nor did he use those obligations ill that love had done him, but turned all his happy moments to the best advantage; and as he knew no vice, his flame aimed at nothing but honour, if such a distinction may be made in love, and especially in that country, where men take to themselves as many as they can maintain and where the only crime and sin with woman is to turn her off, to abandon her to want, shame, and misery. Such ill morals are only practised in Christian countries where they prefer the bare name of religion and, without virtue or morality, think that's sufficient. But Oroonoko was none of those professors; but as he had right notions of honour, so he made her such propositions as were not only and barely such but, contrary to the custom of his country, he made her vows she should be the only woman he would possess while he lived; that no age or wrinkles should incline him to change, for her soul would be always fine and always young, and he should have an eternal idea in his mind of the charms she now bore and should look into his heart for that idea when he could find it no longer in her face.

After a thousand assurances of his lasting flame and her eternal empire over him, she condescended to receive him for her husband; or rather, received him as the greatest honour the gods could do her. There is a certain ceremony in these cases to be observed, which I forgot to ask him how performed; but 'twas concluded on both sides that, in obedience to him, the grandfather was to be first made acquainted with the design, for they pay a most absolute resignation to the monarch, especially when he is a parent also.

On the other side, the old king, who had many wives and many concubines, wanted not court flatterers to insinuate in his heart a thousand tender thoughts for this young beauty, and who represented her to his fancy as the most charming he had ever possessed in all the long race of his numerous years. At this character his old heart, like an extinguished brand most apt to take fire, felt new sparks of love, and began to kindle, and now, grown to his second childhood, longed with impatience to behold this gay thing with whom, alas!, he could but innocently play. But how he should be confirmed she was this wonder, before he used his power to call her to court (where maidens never came unless for the king's private use) he was next to consider, and while he was so doing, he had intelligence brought him that Imoinda was most certainly mistress to the Prince Oroonoko. This gave him some chagrin; however, it gave him also an opportunity, one day, when the prince was a-hunting, to wait on a man of quality as his slave and attendant who should go and make a present to Imoinda, as from the prince; he should then, unknown, see this fair maid and have an opportunity to hear what message she would return the prince for his present, and from thence gather the state of her heart and degree of her inclination. This was put in execution, and the old monarch saw and burnt; he found her all he had heard, and would not delay his happiness, but found he should have some obstacle to overcome her heart, for she expressed her sense of the present the prince had sent her in terms so sweet, so soft and pretty, with an air of love and joy that could not be dissembled, insomuch that 'twas past doubt whether she loved Oroonoko entirely. This gave the old king some affliction, but he salved it with this: that the obedience the people pay their king was not at all inferior to what they paid their gods, and what love would not oblige Imoinda to do, duty would compel her to.

He was therefore no sooner got to his apartment but he sent the royal veil to Imoinda; that is, the ceremony of invitation: he sends the lady he has a mind to honour with his bed a veil, with which she is covered and secured for the king's use and 'tis death to disobey; besides, held a most impious disobedience. 'Tis not to be imagined the surprise and grief that seized this lovely maid at this news and sight. However, as delays in these cases are dangerous, and pleading worse than treason, trembling and almost fainting, she was obliged to suffer herself to be covered and led away.

They brought her thus to court, and the king, who had caused a very rich bath to be prepared, was led into it where he sat under a canopy in state to receive this longed-for virgin, whom he having commanded should be brought to him, they (after disrobing her) led her to the bath and, making fast the doors, left her to descend. The king, without more courtship, bade her throw off her mantle and come to his arms. But Imoinda, all in tears, threw herself on the marble on the brink of the bath and besought him to hear her. She told him, as she was a maid, how proud of the divine glory she should have been of having it in her power to oblige her king, but as by the laws he could not, and from his royal goodness would not, take from any man his wedded wife, so she believed she should be the occasion of making him commit a great sin, if she did not reveal her state and condition, and tell him she was another's, and could not be so happy to be his.

The king, enraged at this delay, hastily demanded the name of the bold man, that had married a woman of her degree without his consent. Imoinda, seeing his eyes fierce and his hands tremble, whether with age or anger I know not, but she fancied the last, almost repented she had said so much, for now she feared the storm would fall on the prince; she therefore said a thousand things to appease the raging of his flame, and to prepare him to hear who it was with calmness, but before she spoke he imagined who she meant, but would not seem to do so, but commanded her to lay aside her mantle and suffer herself to receive his caresses; or, by his gods, he swore that happy man whom she was going to name should die, though it were even Oroonoko himself.

"Therefore," said he, "deny this marriage, and swear thyself a maid."

"That," replied Imoinda, "by all our powers I do, for I am not yet known to my husband."

"'Tis enough," said the king, "'tis enough to satisfy both my conscience and my heart." And rising from his seat, he went and led her into the bath, it being in vain for her to resist.

In this time the prince, who was returned from hunting, went to visit his Imoinda, but found her gone, and not only so, but heard she had received the royal veil. This raised him to a storm and, in his madness, they had much ado to save him from laying violent hands on himself. Force first prevailed, and then reason. They urged all to him that might oppose his rage, but nothing weighed so greatly with him as the king's old age uncapable of injuring him with Imoinda. He would give way to that hope because it pleased him most and flattered best his heart. Yet this served not altogether to make him cease his different passions, which sometimes raged within him, and sometimes softened into showers. 'Twas not enough to appease him, to tell him his grandfather was old, and could not that way injure him, while he retained that aweful duty which the young men are used there to pay to their grave relations. He could not be convinced he had no cause to sigh and mourn for the loss of a mistress he could not with all his strength and courage retrieve. And he would often cry: "O my friends! were she in walled cities, or confined from me in fortifications of the greatest strength, did enchantments or monsters detain her from me, I would venture through any hazard to free her. But here, in the arms of a feeble old man, my youth, my violent love, my trade in arms, and all my vast desire of glory avail me nothing. Imoinda is as irrecoverably lost to me as if she were snatched by the cold arms of death. O she is never to be retrieved! If I would wait tedious years till fate should bow the old king to his grave, even that would not leave me Imoinda free, but still that custom that makes it so vile a crime for a son to marry his father's wives or mistresses would hinder my happiness, unless I would either ignobly set an ill precedent to my successors, or abandon my country and fly with her to some unknown world who never heard our story."

But it was objected to him that his case was not the same, for Imoinda being his lawful wife by solemn contract, 'twas he was the injured man and might, if he so pleased, take Imoinda back, the breach of the law being on his grandfather's side; and that if he could circumvent him and redeem her from the Otan, which is the palace of the king's women, a sort of seraglio, it was both just and lawful for him so to do.

This reasoning had some force upon him, and he should have been entirely comforted but for the thought that she was possessed by his grandfather; however, he loved so well, that he was resolved to believe what most favoured his hope, and to endeavour to learn from Imoinda's own mouth what only she could satisfy him in: whether she was robbed of that blessing which was only due to his faith and love. But as it was very hard to get a sight of the women, for no men ever entered into the Otan, but when the king went to entertain himself with some one of his wives or mistresses, and 'twas death at any other time for any other to go in, so he knew not how to contrive to get a sight of her.

While Oroonoko felt all the agonies of love, and suffered under a torment the most painful in the world, the old king was not ex-empted from his share of affliction. He was troubled for having been forced by an irresistible passion to rob his son of a treasure he knew could not but be extremely dear to him, since she was the most beautiful that ever had been seen, and had besides all the sweetness and innocence of youth and modesty with a charm of wit surpassing all. He found that, however she was forced to expose her lovely person to his withered arms, she could only sigh and weep there and think of Oroonoko, and oftentimes could not forbear speaking of him, though her life were by custom forfeited by own-ing her passion. But she spoke not of a lover only, but of a prince dear to him to whom she spoke, and of the praises of a man who, till now, filled the old man's soul with joy at every recital of his bravery, or even his name. And 'twas this dotage on our young hero that gave Imoinda a thousand privileges to speak of him with-out offending; and this condescension in the old king that made her take the satisfaction of speaking of him so very often.

Besides, he many times enquired how the prince bore himself, and those of whom he asked, being entirely slaves to the merits and virtues of the prince, still answered what they thought conduced best to his service; which was, to make the old king fancy that the prince had no more interest in Imoinda, and had resigned her will-ingly to the pleasure of the king; that he diverted himself with his mathematicians, his fortifications, his officers, and his hunting.

This pleased the old lover, who failed not to report these things again to Imoinda, that she might, by the example of her young lover, withdraw her heart and rest better contented in his arms. But however she was forced to receive this unwelcome news, in all appearance with unconcern and content, her heart was bursting within, and she was only happy when she could get alone to vent her griefs and moans with sighs and tears.

What reports of the prince's conduct were made to the king, he thought good to justify as far as possibly he could by his actions; and when he appeared in the presence of the king, he showed a face not at all betraying his heart: so that in a little time the old man, being entirely convinced that he was no longer a lover of Imoinda, he carried him with him, in his train, to the Otan, often to banquet with his mistress. But as soon as he entered, one day, into the apartment of Imoinda with the king, at the first glance from her eyes, notwithstanding all his determined resolution, he was ready to sink in the place where he stood, and had certainly done so, but for the support of Aboan, a young man who was next to him, which, with his change of countenance, had betrayed him, had the king chanced to look that way. And I have observed, 'tis a very great error in those who laugh when one says a Negro can change colour, for I have seen 'em as frequently blush and look pale, and that as visibly as ever I saw in the most beautiful white. And 'tis certain that both these changes were evident this day in both these lovers. And Imoinda, who saw with some joy the change in the prince's face, and found it in her own, strove to divert the king from beholding either by a forced caress, with which she met him; which was a new wound in the heart of the poor dying prince. But as soon as the king was busied in looking on some fine thing of Imoinda's making, she had time to tell the prince with her angry but love-darting eyes that she resented his coldness, and bemoaned her own miserable captivity. Nor were his eyes silent, but answered hers again, as much as eyes could do, instructed by the most tender, and most passionate heart that ever loved; and they spoke so well and so effectually, as Imoinda no longer doubted but she was the only delight and the darling of that soul she found pleading in 'em its right of love, which none was more willing to resign than she. And 'twas this powerful language alone that in an instant conveyed all the thoughts of their souls to each other, that they both found there wanted but opportunity to make them both entirely happy.

But when he saw another door opened by Onahal, a former old wife of the king's, who now had charge of Imoinda, and saw the prospect of a bed of state made ready with sweets and flowers for the dalliance of the king, who immediately led the trembling victim from his sight into that prepared repose, what rage, what wild frenzies seized his heart, which forcing to keep within bounds, and to suffer without noise, it became the more insupportable, and rent his soul with ten thousand pains. He was forced to retire to vent his groans, where he fell down on a carpet and lay struggling a long time, and only breathing now and then, "O Imoinda!". When Onahal had finished her necessary affair within, shutting the door, she came forth to wait till the king called, and hearing someone sighing in the other room, she passed on, and found the prince in that deplorable condition, which she thought needed her aid. She gave him cordials, but all in vain, till finding the nature of his disease by his sighs and naming Imoinda, she told him he had not so much cause as he imagined to afflict himself, for if he knew the king so well as she did, he would not lose a moment in jealousy, and that she was confident that Imoinda bore at this minute part in his affliction. Aboan was of the same opinion, and both together persuaded him to reassume his courage, and all sitting down on the carpet, the prince said so many obliging things to Onahal, that he half persuaded her to be of his party. And she promised him she would thus far comply with his just desires that she would let Imoinda know how faithful he was, what he suffered, and what he said.

This discourse lasted till the king called, which gave Oroonoko a certain satisfaction, and with the hope Onahal had made him conceive, he assumed a look as gay as 'twas possible a man in his circumstances could do, and presently after, he was called in with the rest who waited without. The king commanded music to be brought, and several of his young wives and mistresses came altogether by his command to dance before him, where Imoinda performed her part with an air and grace so passing all the rest as her beauty was above 'em, and received the present ordained as a prize. The prince was every moment more charmed with the new beauties and graces he beheld in this fair one, and while he gazed and she danced, Onahal was retired to a window with Aboan.

This Onahal, as I said, was one of the cast-mistresses of the old king, and 'twas these (now past their beauty) that were made guardians or governants to the new and the young ones and whose business it was to teach them all those wanton arts of love with which they prevailed and charmed heretofore in their turn, and who now treated the triumphing happy ones with all the severity, as to liberty and freedom, that was possible, in revenge of those honours they robbed them of, envying them those satisfactions, those gallantries, and presents that were once made to themselves while youth and beauty lasted, and which they now saw pass regardless by, and paid only to the bloomings. And certainly nothing is more afflicting to a decayed beauty than to behold in itself declining charms that were once adored and to find those caresses paid to new beauties, to which once she laid a claim; to hear 'em whisper as she passes by, "That once was a delicate woman." These abandoned ladies therefore endeavour to revenge all the despites and decays of time on these flourishing happy ones. And 'twas this severity that gave Oroonoko a thousand fears he should never prevail with Onahal to see Imoinda. But, as I said, she was now retired to a window with Aboan.

This young man was not only one of the best quality, but a man extremely well made and beautiful; and coming often to attend the king to the Otan, he had subdued the heart of the antiquated Onahal, which had not forgot how pleasant it was to be in love. And though she had some decays in her face, she had none in her sense and wit; she was there agreeable still, even to Aboan's youth, so that he took pleasure in entertaining her with discourses of love. He knew also that to make his court to these she-favourites was the way to be great, these being the persons that do all affairs and business at court. He had also observed that she had given him glances more tender and inviting than she had done to others of his quality and now, when he saw that her favour could so absolutely oblige the prince, he failed not to sigh in her ear, and to look with eyes all soft upon her, and give her hope that she had made some impressions on his heart. He found her pleased at this and making a thousand advances to him, but the ceremony ending and the king departing broke up the company for that day and his conversation.

Aboan failed not that night to tell the prince of his success and how advantageous the service of Onahal might be to his amour with Imoinda. The prince was overjoyed with this good news, and besought him if it were possible to caress her so as to engage her entirely; which he could not fail to do if he complied with her desires. "For then," said the prince, "her life lying at your mercy, she must grant you the request you make in my behalf." Aboan understood him and assured him he would make love so effectually that he would defy the most expert mistress of the art to find out whether he dissembled it, or had it really. And 'twas with impatience they waited the next opportunity of going to the Otan.

The wars came on, the time of taking the field approached, and 'twas impossible for the prince to delay his going at the head of his army, to encounter the enemy, so that every day seemed a tedious year till he saw his Imoinda; for he believed he could not live if he were forced away without being so happy. 'Twas with impatience, therefore, that he expected the next visit the king would make, and, according to his wish, it was not long. The parley of the eyes of these two lovers had not passed so secretly, but an old jealous lover could spy it; or rather, he wanted not flatterers who told him they observed it. So that the prince was hastened to the camp and this was the last visit he found he should make to the Otan. He therefore urged Aboan to make the best of this last effort, and to explain himself so to Onahal that she, deferring her enjoyment of her young lover no longer, might make way for the prince to speak to Imoinda.

The whole affair being agreed on between the prince and Aboan, they attended the king, as the custom was, to the Otan; where, while the whole company was taken up in beholding the dancing, and antic postures the women royal made to divert the king, Onahal singled out Aboan, whom she found most pliable to her wish. When she had him where she believed she could not be heard, she sighed to him, and softly cried: "Ah, Aboan! When will you be sensible of my passion? I confess it with my mouth, because I would not give my eyes the lie and you have but too much already perceived they have confessed my flame; nor would I have you believe that because I am the abandoned mistress of a king, I esteem myself altogether divested of charms. No, Aboan, I have still a rest of beauty enough engaging, and have learned to please too well not to be desirable. I can have lovers still, but will have none but Aboan."

"Madam," replied the half-feigning youth, "you have already, by my eyes, found you can still conquer; and I believe 'tis in pity of me you condescend to this kind confession. But, Madam, words are used to be so small a part of our country courtship, that 'tis rare one can get so happy an opportunity as to tell one's heart; and those few minutes we have are forced to be snatched for more certain fruits of love than speaking and sighing and such I languish for."

He spoke this with such a tone that she hoped it true, and could not forbear believing it; and being wholly transported with joy, for having subdued the finest of all the king's subjects to her desires, she took from her ears two large pearls and commanded him to wear 'em in his. He would have refused 'em, crying, "Madam, these are not the proofs of your love that I expect; 'tis opportunity, 'tis a lone hour only that can make me happy." But forcing the pearls into his hand, she whispered softly to him, "O do not fear a woman's invention when love sets her a-thinking." And pressing his hand she cried, "This night you shall be happy. Come to the gate of the orange groves behind the Otan and I will be ready about midnight to receive you."

"'Twas thus agreed, and she left him, that no notice might be taken of their speaking together. The ladies were still dancing and the king, laid on a carpet, with a great deal of pleasure was beholding them, especially Imoinda, who that day appeared more lovely than ever, being enlivened with the good tidings Onahal had brought her of the constant passion the prince had for her. The prince was laid on another carpet at the other end of the room, with his eyes fixed on the object of his soul; and as she turned, or moved, so did they, and she alone gave his eyes and soul their motions; nor did Imoinda employ her eyes to any other use than in beholding with infinite pleasure the joy she produced in those of the prince. But while she was more regarding him than the steps she took, she chanced to fall, and so near him as that, leaping with extreme force from the carpet, he caught her in his arms as she fell, and 'twas visible to the whole presence the joy wherewith he received her. He clasped her close to his bosom and quite forgot that reverence that was due to the mistress of a king, and that punishment that is the reward of a boldness of this nature; and had not the presence of mind of Imoinda (fonder of his safety than her own) befriended him, in making her spring from his arms and fall into her dance again, he had, at that instant, met his death; for the old king, jealous to the last degree, rose up in rage, broke all the diversion and led Imoinda to her apartment, and sent out word to the prince to go immediately to the camp and that if he were found another night in court he should suffer the death ordained for disobedient offenders.

You may imagine how welcome this news was to Oroonoko, whose unseasonable transport and caress of Imoinda was blamed by all men that loved him; and now he perceived his fault, yet cried that for such another moment he would be content to die.

All the Otan was in disorder about this accident, and Onahal was particularly concerned because on the prince's stay depended her happiness, for she could no longer expect that of Aboan. So that, ere they departed, they contrived it so that the prince and he should come both that night to the grove of the Otan, which was all of oranges and citrons, and that there they should wait her orders.

They parted thus, with grief enough, till night, leaving the king in possession of the lovely maid. But nothing could appease the jealousy of the old lover. He would not be imposed on, but would have it that Imoinda made a false step on purpose to fall into Oroonoko's bosom, and that all things looked like a design on both sides, and 'twas in vain she protested her innocence: he was old and obstinate and left her more than half assured that his fear was true.

The king, going to his apartment, sent to know where the prince was, and if he intended to obey his command. The messenger returned, and told him he found the prince pensive and altogether unpreparing for the campaign; that he lay negligently on the ground and answered very little. This confirmed the jealousy of the king, and he commanded that they should very narrowly and privately watch his motions, and that he should not stir from his apartment, but one spy or other should be employed to watch him. So that the hour approaching wherein he was to go to the citron grove, and taking only Aboan along with him, he leaves his apartment and was watched to the very gate of the Otan, where he was seen to enter, and where they left him to carry back the tidings to the king.

Oroonoko and Aboan were no sooner entered, but Onahal led the prince to the apartment of Imoinda; who, not knowing anything of her happiness, was laid in bed. But Onahal only left him in her chamber to make the best of his opportunity, and took her dear Aboan to her own, where he showed the height of complaisance for his prince when, to give him an opportunity, he suffered himself to be caressed in bed by Onahal.

The prince softly wakened Imoinda, who was not a little surprised with joy to find him there, and yet she trembled with a thousand fears. I believe he omitted saying nothing to this young maid that might persuade her to suffer him to seize his own, and take the rights of love; and I believe she was not long resisting those arms, where she so longed to be; and having opportunity, night, and silence, youth, love, and desire, he soon prevailed and ravished in a moment what his old grandfather had been endeavouring for so many months.

'Tis not to be imagined the satisfaction of these two young lovers, nor the vows she made him, that she remained a spotless maid till that night, and that what she did with his grandfather had robbed him of no part of her virgin honour, the gods, in mercy and justice, having reserved that for her plighted Lord, to whom of right it belonged. And 'tis impossible to express the transports he suffered, while he listened to a discourse so charming from her loved lips and clasped that body in his arms for whom he had so long languished; and nothing now afflicted him but his sudden departure from her, for he told her the necessity, and his commands; but should depart satisfied in this, that since the old king had hitherto not been able to deprive him of those enjoyments which only belonged to him, he believed for the future he would be less able to injure him; so that, abating the scandal of the veil, which was no otherwise so, than that she was wife to another, he believed her safe, even in the arms of the king, and innocent—yet would he have ventured at the conquest of the world, and have given it all, to have had her avoided that honour of receiving the royal veil. 'Twas thus, between a thousand caresses, that both bemoaned the hard fate of youth and beauty, so liable to that cruel promotion. 'Twas a glory that could well have been spared here, though desired and aimed at by all the young females of that kingdom.

But while they were thus fondly employed, forgetting how time ran on, and that the dawn must conduct him far away from his only happiness, they heard a great noise in the Otan, and unusual voices of men, at which the prince, starting from the arms of the frighted Imoinda, ran to a little battleaxe he used to wear by his side, and having not so much leisure as to put on his habit, he opposed himself against some who were already opening the door, which they did with so much violence that Oroonoko was not able to defend it, but was forced to cry out with a commanding voice, "Whoever ye are that have the boldness to attempt to approach this apartment thus rudely, know, that I, the Prince Oroonoko, will revenge it with the certain death of him that first enters. Therefore stand back and know this place is sacred to love and me this night; tomorrow 'tis the king's."

This he spoke with a voice so resolved and assured that they soon retired from the door, but cried, "'Tis by the king's command we are come, and being satisfied by thy voice, O Prince, as much as if we had entered, we can report to the king the truth of all his fears, and leave thee to provide for thy own safety, as thou art advised by thy friends."

At these words they departed, and left the prince to take a short and sad leave of his Imoinda, who trusting in the strength of her charms, believed she should appease the fury of a jealous king by saying she was surprised, and that it was by force of arms he got into her apartment. All her concern now was for his life, and therefore she hastened him to the camp, and with much ado prevailed on him to go. Nor was it she alone that prevailed: Aboan and Onahal both pleaded and both assured him of a lie that should be well enough contrived to secure Imoinda. So that at last, with a heart sad as death, dying eyes, and sighing soul, Oroonoko departed and took his way to the camp.

It was not long after the king in person came to the Otan, where beholding Imoinda with rage in his eyes, he upbraided her wickedness and perfidy, and threatening her royal lover—she fell on her face at his feet, bedewing the floor with her tears, and imploring his pardon for a fault which she had not with her will committed, as Onahal, who was also prostrate with her, could testify: that, unknown to her, he had broke into her apartment and ravished her. She spoke this much against her conscience, but to save her own life, 'twas absolutely necessary she should feign this falsity. She knew it could not injure the prince, he being fled to an army that would stand by him against any injuries that should assault him. However, this last thought of Imoinda's being ravished changed the measures of his revenge; and whereas before he designed to be himself her executioner, he now resolved she should not die. But as it is the greatest crime in nature amongst 'em to touch a woman, after having been possessed by a son, a father, or a brother, so now he looked on Imoinda as a polluted thing, wholly unfit for his embrace; nor would he resign her to his grandson, because she had received the royal veil. He therefore removes her from the Otan with Onahal, whom he put into safe hands, with order they should be both sold off as slaves to another country, either Christian or heathen, 'twas no matter where.

This cruel sentence, worse than death, they implored might be reversed; but their prayers were vain, and it was put in execution accordingly, and that with so much secrecy, that none, either without or within the Otan, knew anything of their absence or their destiny. The old king, nevertheless, executed this with a great deal of reluctancy, but he believed he had made a very great conquest over himself, when he had once resolved, and had performed what he resolved. He believed now that his love had been unjust, and that he could not expect the gods, or captain of the clouds (as they call the unknown power), should suffer a better consequence from so ill a cause. He now begins to hold Oroonoko excused, and to say he had reason for what he did; and now everybody could assure the king how passionately Imoinda was beloved by the prince, even those confessed it now who said the contrary before his flame was abated. So that the king being old, and not able to defend himself in war, and having no sons of all his race remaining alive, but only this to maintain him on his throne, and looking on this as a man disobliged, first by the rape of his mistress, or rather, wife, and now by depriving of him wholly of her, he feared might make him desperate, and do some cruel thing either to himself or his old grandfather, the offender. He began to repent him extremely of the contempt he had, in his rage, put on Imoinda. Besides, he considered he ought in honour to have killed her for this offence—if it had been one. He ought to have had so much value and consideration for a maid of her quality, as to have nobly put her to death, and not to have sold her like a common slave, the greatest revenge and the most disgraceful of any, and to which they a thousand times prefer death and implore it, as Imoinda did, but could not obtain that honour. Seeing therefore it was certain that Oroonoko would highly resent this affront, he thought good to make some excuse for his rashness to him, and to that end he sent a messenger to the camp, with orders to treat with him about the matter, to gain his pardon, and to endeavour to mitigate his grief; but that by no means he should tell him she was sold, but secretly put to death, for he knew he should never obtain his pardon for the other.

When the messenger came, he found the prince upon the point of engaging with the enemy, but as soon as he heard of the arrival of the messenger, he commanded him to his tent, where he embraced him, and received him with joy, which was soon abated by the downcast looks of the messenger, who was instantly demanded the cause by Oroonoko, who, impatient of delay, asked a thousand questions in a breath, and all concerning Imoinda. But there needed little return, for he could almost answer himself of all he demanded from his sighs and eyes. At last, the messenger casting himself at the prince's feet and kissing them with all the submission of a man that had something to implore which he dreaded to utter, he besought him to hear with calmness what he had to deliver to him, and to call up all his noble and heroic courage to encounter with his words, and defend himself against the ungrateful things he must relate. Oroonoko replied with a deep sigh and a languishing voice, "—I am armed against their worst efforts—for I know they will tell me Imoinda is no more—and after that, you may spare the rest." Then commanding him to rise, he laid himself on a carpet under a rich pavilion, and remained a good while silent, and was hardly heard to sigh. When he was come a little to himself, the messenger asked him leave to deliver that part of his embassy, which the prince had not yet divined, and the prince cried, "I permit thee—" Then he told him the affliction the old king was in for the rashness he had committed in his cruelty to Imoinda, and how he deigned to ask pardon for his offence, and to implore the prince would not suffer that loss to touch his heart too sensibly, which now all the gods could not restore him, but might recompense him in glory, which he begged he would pursue; and that death, that common revenger of all injuries, would soon even the account between him and a feeble old man.

Oroonoko bade him return his duty to his lord and master, and to assure him, there was no account of revenge to be adjusted between them; if there were, 'twas he was the aggressor, and that death would be just and, maugre his age, would see him righted; and he was contented to leave his share of glory to youths more fortunate and worthy of that favour from the gods. That henceforth he would never lift a weapon or draw a bow, but abandon the small remains of his life to sighs and tears, and the continual thoughts of what his lord and grandfather had thought good to send out of the world, with all that youth, that innocence, and beauty.

After having spoken this, whatever his greatest officers and men of the best rank could do, they could not raise him from the carpet or persuade him to action and resolutions of life, but commanding all to retire, he shut himself into his pavilion all that day, while the enemy was ready to engage, and wondering at the delay, the whole body of the chief of the army then addressed themselves to him, and to whom they had much ado to get admittance. They fell on their faces at the foot of his carpet, where they lay, and besought him with earnest prayers and tears to lead 'em forth to battle, and not let the enemy take advantages of them, and implored him to have regard to his glory, and to the world, that depended on his courage and conduct. But he made no other reply to all their supplications but this: that he had now no more business for glory; and for the world, it was a trifle not worth his care.

"Go," continued he, sighing, "and divide it amongst you, and reap with joy what you so vainly prize, and leave me to my more welcome destiny."

They then demanded what they should do, and whom he would constitute in his room, that the confusion of ambitious youth and power might not ruin their order, and make them a prey to the enemy. He replied, he would not give himself the trouble—but wished 'em to choose the bravest man amongst 'em, let his quality or birth be what it would. "For, O my friends," said he, "it is not titles make men brave, or good, or birth that bestows courage and generosity, or makes the owner happy. Believe this, when you behold Oroonoko, the most wretched and abandoned by fortune of all the creation of the gods." So turning himself about, he would make no more reply to all they could urge or implore.

The army, beholding their officers return unsuccessful, with sad faces and ominous looks that presaged no good luck, suffered a thousand fears to take possession of their hearts, and the enemy to come even upon 'em before they would provide for their safety by any defence; and though they were assured by some, who had a mind to animate 'em, that they should be immediately headed by the prince, and that in the mean time Aboan had orders to command as general, yet they were so dismayed for want of that great example of bravery, that they could make but a very feeble resistance, and at last, downright fled before the enemy, who pursued 'em to the very tents, killing 'em. Nor could all Aboan's courage, which that day gained him immortal glory, shame 'em into a manly defence of themselves. The guards that were left behind about the prince's tent, seeing the soldiers flee before the enemy, and scatter themselves all over the plain in great disorder, made such outcries as roused the prince from his amorous slumber, in which he had remained buried for two days without permitting any sustenance to approach him. But, in spite of all his resolutions, he had not the constancy of grief to that degree as to make him insensible of the danger of his army, and in that instant he leaped from his couch and cried, "Come, if we must die, let us meet death the noblest way; and 'twill be more like Oroonoko to encounter him at an army's head, opposing the torrent of a conquering foe, than lazily on a couch to wait his lingering pleasure and die every moment by a thousand wrecking thought[s]; or be tamely taken by an enemy and led a whining, love-sick slave, to adorn the triumphs of Jamoan, that young victor, who already is entered beyond the limits I had prescribed him."

While he was speaking he suffered his people to dress him for the field; and sallying out of his pavilion, with more life and vigour in his countenance than ever he showed, he appeared like some divine power descended to save his country from destruction and his people had purposely put him on all things that might make him shine with most splendour, to strike a reverent awe into the beholders. He flew into the thickest of those that were pursuing his men, and being animated with despair, he fought as if he came on purpose to die, and did such things as will not be believed that human strength could perform, and such as soon inspired all the rest with new courage and new order. And now it was that they began to fight indeed, and so, as if they would not be outdone, even by their adored hero, who turning the tide of the victory, changing absolutely the fate of the day, gained an entire conquest, and Oroonoko, having the good fortune to single out Jamoan, he took him prisoner with his own hand, having wounded him almost to death.

This Jamoan afterwards became very dear to him, being a man very gallant, and of excellent graces, and fine parts; so that he never put him amongst the rank of captives, as they used to do, without distinction, for the common sale or market, but kept him in his own court, where he retained nothing of the prisoner but the name, and returned no more into his own country, so great an affection he took for Oroonoko, and by a thousand tales and adventures of love and gallantry, flattered his disease of melancholy and languishment, which I have often heard him say, had certainly killed him but for the conversation of this prince and Aboan, and the French governor he had from his childhood, of whom I have spoken before, and who was a man of admirable wit, great ingenuity, and learning, all which he had infused into his young pupil. This Frenchman was banished out of his own country for some heretical notions he held, and though he was a man of very little religion, he had admirable morals, and a brave soul.

After the total defeat of Jamoan's army, which all fled, or were left dead upon the place, they spent some time in the camp, Oroonoko choosing rather to remain a while there in his tents, than enter into a place, or live in a court where he had so lately suffered so great a loss. The officers therefore who saw and knew his cause of discontent, invented all sorts of diversions and sports to entertain their prince. So that what with those amusements abroad, and others at home—that is, within their tents—with the persuasions, arguments, and care of his friends and servants that he more peculiarly prized, he wore off in time a great part of that chagrin and torture of despair which the first efforts of Imoinda's death had given him, insomuch as having received a thousand kind embassies from the king, and invitations to return to court, he obeyed, though with no little reluctancy, and when he did so, there was a visible change in him, and for a long time he was much more melancholy than before. But time lessens all extremes and reduces 'em to mediums and unconcern; but no motives or beauties, though all endeavoured it, could engage him in any sort of amour, though he had all the invitations to it, both from his own youth and others' ambitions and designs.

Oroonoko was no sooner returned from this last conquest, and received at court with all the joy and magnificence that could be expressed to a young victor who was not only returned triumphant, but beloved like a deity, when there arrived in the port an English ship. This person had often before been in these countries, and was very well known to Oroonoko, with whom he had trafficked for slaves, and had used to do the same with his predecessors. This commander was a man of a finer sort of address and conversation, better bred and more engaging than most of that sort of men are, so that he seemed rather never to have been bred out of a court, than almost all his life at sea. This captain therefore was always better received at court than most of the traders to those countries were, and especially by Oroonoko, who was more civilized, according to the European mode, than any other had been, and took more delight in the white nations and, above all, men of parts and wit. To this captain he sold abundance of his slaves, and for the favour and esteem he had for him, made him many presents, and obliged him to stay at court as long as possibly he could, which the captain seemed to take as a very great honour done him, entertaining the prince every day with globes and maps and mathematical discourses and instruments, eating, drinking, hunting, and living with him with so much familiarity that it was not to be doubted but he had gained very greatly upon the heart of this gallant young man. And the captain, in return of all these mighty favours, besought the prince to honour his vessel with his presence some day or other to dinner before he should set sail, which he condescended to accept and appointed his day. The captain, on his part, failed not to have all things in a readiness in the most magnificent order he could possibly. And the day being come, the captain in his boat, richly adorned with carpets and velvet cushions, rowed to the shore to receive the prince, with another long boat, where was placed all his music and trumpets, with which Oroonoko was extremely delighted, who met him on the shore, attended by his French governor, Jamoan, Aboan, and about an hundred of the noblest youths of the court. And after they had first carried the prince on board, the boats fetched the rest off, where they found a very splendid treat, with all sorts of fine wines, and were as well entertained as 'twas possible in such a place to be.

The prince, having drunk hard of punch, and several sorts of wine, as did all the rest (for great care was taken they should want nothing of that part of the entertainment), was very merry and in great admiration of the ship, for he had never been in one before, so that he was curious of beholding every place where he decently might descend. The rest, no less curious, who were not quite overcome with drinking, rambled at their pleasure fore and aft, as their fancies guided 'em. So that the captain, who had well laid his design before, gave the word and seized on all his guests, they clapping great irons suddenly on the prince, when he was leaped down in the hold to view that part of the vessel, and locking him fast down, secured him. The same treachery was used to all the rest, and all in one instant, in several places of the ship, were lashed fast in irons and betrayed to slavery. That great design over, they set all hands to work to hoist sail, and with as treacherous and fair a wind, they made from the shore with this innocent and glorious prize, who thought of nothing less than such an entertainment.

Some have commended this act as brave in the captain, but I will spare my sense of it, and leave it to my reader to judge as he pleases. It may be easily guessed in what manner the prince resented this indignity, who may be best resembled to a lion taken in a toil; so he raged, so he struggled for liberty, but all in vain, and they had so wisely managed his fetters that he could not use a hand in his defence to quit himself of a life that would by no means endure slavery, nor could he move from the place where he was tied to any solid part of the ship, against which he might have beat his head, and have finished his disgrace that way. So that being deprived of all other means, he resolved to perish for want of food, and pleased at last with that thought, and toiled and tired by rage and indignation, he laid himself down and sullenly resolved upon dying, and refused all things that were brought him. This did not a little vex the captain, and the more so because he found almost all of 'em of the same humour, so that the loss of so many brave slaves, so tall and goodly to behold, would have been very considerable. He therefore ordered one to go from him (for he would not be seen himself) to Oroonoko, and to assure him he was afflicted for having rashly done so unhospitable a deed, and which could not be now remedied, since they were far from shore. But since he resented it in so high a nature, he assured him he would revoke his resolution, and set both him and his friends ashore in the next land they should touch at, and of this the messenger gave him his oath, provided he would resolve to live. And Oroonoko, whose honour was such as he never had violated a word in his life himself, much less a solemn asseveration, believed in an instant what this man said, but replied, he expected for a confirmation of this to have his shameful fetters dismissed. This demand was carried to the captain, who returned him answer that the offence had been so great which he had put upon the prince, that he durst not trust him with liberty while he remained in the ship, for fear lest by a valour natural to him, and a revenge that would animate that valour, he might commit some outrage fatal to himself and the King his master, to whom his vessel did belong. To this Oroonoko replied, he would engage his honour to behave himself in all friendly order and manner, and obey the command of the captain as he was lord of the King's vessel, and general of those men under his command.

This was delivered to the still-doubting captain, who could not resolve to trust a heathen, he said, upon his parole, a man that had no sense or notion of the god that he worshipped. Oroonoko then replied, he was very sorry to hear that the captain pretended to the knowledge and worship of any gods who had taught him no better principles than not to credit as he would be credited; but they told him the difference of their faith occasioned that distrust, for the captain had protested to him upon the word of a Christian, and sworn in the name of a great god, which if he should violate, he would expect eternal torment in the world to come. "Is that all the obligation he has to be just to his oath?," replied Oroonoko. "Let him know I swear by my honour, which to violate would not only render me contemptible and despised by all brave and honest men, and so give myself perpetual pain, but it would be eternally offending and diseasing all mankind, harming, betraying, circumventing, and outraging all men; but punishments hereafter are suffered by oneself, and the world takes no cognisances whether this god have revenged 'em or not, 'tis done so secretly, and deferred so long, while the man of no honour suffers every moment the scorn and contempt of the honester world, and dies every day ignominiously in his fame, which is more valuable than life. I speak not this to move belief, but to show you how you mistake, when you imagine that he who will violate his honour will keep his word with his gods."

So turning from him with a disdainful smile, he refused to answer him when he urged him to know what answer he should carry back to his captain, so that he departed without saying any more. The captain pondering and consulting what to do, it was concluded that nothing but Oroonoko's liberty would encourage any of the rest to eat, except the Frenchman, whom the captain could not pretend to keep prisoner, but only told him he was secured because he might act something in favour of the prince, but that he should be freed as soon as they came to land. So that they concluded it wholly necessary to free the prince from his irons, that he might show himself to the rest, that they might have an eye upon him, and that they could not fear a single man.

This being resolved, to make the obligation the greater, the captain himself went to Oroonoko, where, after many compliments and assurances of what he had already promised, he, receiving from the prince his parole and his hand for his good behaviour, dismissed his irons and brought him to his own cabin, where, after having treated and reposed him a while, for he had neither eat nor slept in four days before, he besought him to visit those obstinate people in chains, who refused all manner of sustenance, and entreated him to oblige 'em to eat, and assure 'em of their liberty the first opportunity.

Oroonoko, who was too generous not to give credit to his words, showed himself to his people, who were transported with excess of joy at the sight of their darling prince, falling at his feet, and kissing and embracing 'em, believing as some divine oracle all he assured 'em. But he besought 'em to bear their chains with that bravery that became those whom he had seen act so nobly in arms, and that they could not give him greater proofs of their love and friendship, since 'twas all the security the captain (his friend) could have, against the revenge, he said, they might possibly justly take for the injuries sustained by him. And they all, with one accord, assured him, they could not suffer enough when it was for his repose and safety.

After this they no longer refused to eat, but took what was brought 'em, and were pleased with their captivity, since by it they hoped to redeem the prince, who, all the rest of the voyage, was treated with all the respect due to his birth, though nothing could divert his melancholy, and he would often sigh for Imoinda, and think this a punishment due to his misfortune in having left that noble maid behind him that fatal night in the Otan, when he fled to the camp.

Possessed with a thousand thoughts of past joys with this fair young person, and a thousand griefs for her eternal loss, he endured a tedious voyage, and at last arrived at the mouth of the river of Surinam, a colony belonging to the King of England, and where they were to deliver some part of their slaves. There the merchants and gentlemen of the country going on board to demand those lots of slaves they had already agreed on, and, amongst those, the overseers of those plantations where I then chanced to be, the captain, who had given the word, ordered his men to bring up those noble slaves in fetters whom I have spoken of, and having put 'em, some in one, and some in other lots with women and children (which they call piccaninnies), they sold 'em off as slaves to several merchants and gentlemen, not putting any two in one lot, because they would separate 'em far from each other, not daring to trust 'em together, lest rage and courage should put 'em upon contriving some great action to the ruin of the colony.

Oroonoko was first seized on, and sold to our overseer, who had the first lot, with seventeen more of all sorts and sizes, but not one of quality with him. When he saw this, he found what they meant; for, as I said, he understood English pretty well, and being wholly unarmed and defenceless, so as it was in vain to make any resistance, he only beheld the captain with a look all fierce and disdainful, upbrading him with eyes that forced blushes on his guilty cheeks. He only cried, in passing over the side of the ship, "Farewell, Sir. 'Tis worth my suffering to gain so true a knowledge both of you and of your gods by whom you swear." And desiring those that held him to forbear their pains, and telling 'em he would make no resistance, he cried, "Come, my fellow slaves, let us descend and see if we can meet with more honour and honesty in the next world we shall touch upon." So he nimbly leaped into the boat and, showing no more concern, suffered himself to be rowed up the river with his seventeen companions.

The gentleman that bought him was a young Cornish gentleman whose name was Trefry, a man of great wit and fine learning and was carried into those parts by the lord governor to manage all his affairs. He, reflecting on the last words of Oroonoko to the captain, and beholding the richness of his vest, no sooner came into the boat but he fixed his eyes on him, and finding something so extraordinary in his face, his shape, and mien, a greatness of look and haughtiness in his air, and finding he spoke English, had a great mind to be inquiring into his quality and fortune; which, though Oroonoko endeavoured to hide by only confessing he was above the rank of common slaves, Trefry soon found he was yet something greater than he confessed, and from that moment began to conceive so vast an esteem for him, that he ever after loved him as his dearest brother, and showed him all the civilities due to so great a man.

Trefry was a very good mathematician and a linguist, could speak French and Spanish, and in the three days they remained in the boat (for so long were they going from the ship to the plantation) he entertained Oroonoko so agreeably with his art and discourse, that he was no less pleased with Trefry than he was with the prince; and he thought himself at least fortunate in this: that since he was a slave, as long as he would suffer himself to remain so, he had a man of so excellent wit and parts for a master. So that before they had finished their voyage up the river, he made no scruple of declaring to Trefry all his fortunes and most part of what I have here related, and put himself wholly into the hands of his new friend, whom he found resenting all the injuries were done him, and was charmed with all the greatness of his actions, which were recited with that modesty and delicate sense, as wholly vanquished him and subdued him to his interest. And he promised him on his word and honour he would find the means to reconduct him to his own country

again, assuring him he had a perfect abhorrence of so dishonourable
an action, and that he would sooner have died, than have been the
author of such a perfidy. He found the prince was very much concerned to know what became of his friends, and how they took
their slavery, and Trefry promised to take care about the enquiring
after their condition, and that he should have an account of 'em.

Though, as Oroonoko afterwards said, he had little reason to
credit the words of a Backearary, yet he knew not why, but he saw
a kind of sincerity and aweful truth in the face of Trefry; he saw an
honesty in his eyes, and he found him wise and witty enough to
understand honour, for it was one of his maxims: a man of wit
could not be a knave or villain.

In their passage up the river, they put in at several houses for
refreshment, and ever when they landed, numbers of people would
flock to behold this man, not but their eyes were daily entertained
with the sight of slaves, but the fame of Oroonoko was gone before
him, and all people were in admiration of his beauty. Besides, he
had a rich habit on, in which he was taken, so different from the
rest, and which the captain could not strip him of, because he was
forced to surprise his person in the minute he sold him. When he
found his habit made him liable, as he thought, to be gazed at the
more, he begged Trefry to give him something more befitting a
slave, which he did, and took off his robes. Nevertheless, he shone
through all, and his osenbrigs (a sort of brown Holland suit he had
on) could not conceal the graces of his looks and mien; and he had
no less admirers than when he had his dazzling habit on; the royal
youth appeared in spite of the slave, and people could not help
treating him after a different manner, without designing it. As soon
as they approached him, they venerated and esteemed him; his eyes
insensibly commanded respect, and his behaviour insinuated it into
every soul, so that there was nothing talked of but this young and
gallant slave, even by those who yet knew not that he was a prince.

I ought to tell you, that the Christians never buy any slaves but
they give 'em some name of their own, their native ones being
likely very barbarous and hard to pronounce; so that Mr Trefry
gave Oroonoko that of Caesar, which name will live in that country as long as that (scarce more) glorious one of the great Roman,
for 'tis most evident he wanted no part of the personal courage of
that Caesar, and acted things as memorable, had they been done in
some part of the world replenished with people and historians that

might have given him his due. But his misfortune was to fall in an obscure world, that afforded only a female pen to celebrate his fame; though I doubt not but it had lived from others' endeavours, if the Dutch, who, immediately after his time, took that country, had not killed, banished and dispersed all those that were capable of giving the world this great man's life much better than I have done. And Mr Trefry, who designed it, died before he began it, and bemoaned himself for not having undertook it in time.

For the future, therefore, I must call Oroonoko Caesar, since by that name only he was known in our Western world, and by that name he was received on shore at Parham House, where he was destined a slave. But if the King himself (God bless him) had come ashore, there could not have been greater expectations by all the whole plantation, and those neighbouring ones, than was on ours at that time, and he was received more like a governor than a slave. Notwithstanding, as the custom was, they assigned him his portion of land, his house, and his business up in the plantation. But as it was more for form than any design to put him to his task, he endured no more of the slave but the name, and remained some days in the house, receiving all visits that were made him without stirring towards that part of the plantation where the Negroes were.

At last, he would needs go view his land, his house and the business assigned him. But he no sooner came to the houses of the slaves, which are like a little town by itself, the Negroes all having left work, but they all came forth to behold him, and found he was that prince who had at several times sold most of 'em to these parts; and, from a veneration they pay to great men, especially if they know 'em, and from the surprise and awe they had at the sight of him, they all cast themselves at his feet, crying out in their language: "Live, O King, long live, O King!," and kissing his feet, paid him even divine homage. Several English gentlemen were with him, and what Mr Trefry had told 'em was here confirmed, of which he himself before had no other witness than Caesar himself. But he was infinitely glad to find his grandeur confirmed by the adoration of all the slaves.

Caesar, troubled with their overjoy, and overceremony, besought 'em to rise, and to receive him as their fellow-slave, assuring them he was no better. At which they set up with one accord a most terrible and hideous mourning and condoling, which he and the English had much ado to appease; but at last they prevailed with 'em, and they prepared all their barbarous music, and everyone killed and dressed something of his own stock (for every family has their land apart on which, at their leisure times, they breed all eatable things) and clubbing it together, made a most magnificent supper, inviting their grandee captain, their prince, to honour it with his presence, which he did, and several English with him, where they all waited on him, some playing, others dancing before him all the time according to the manners of their several nations, and with unwearied industry endeavouring to please and delight him.

While they sat at meat, Mr Trefry told Caesar that most of these young slaves were undone in love with a fine she-slave, whom they had had about six months on their land; the prince, who never heard the name of love without a sigh, nor any mention of it without the curiosity of examining further into that tale, which of all discourses was most agreeable to him, asked how they came to be so unhappy as to be all undone for one fair slave. Trefry, who was naturally amorous, and loved to talk of love as well as anybody, proceeded to tell him they had the most charming Black that ever was beheld on their plantation, about fifteen or sixteen years old, as he guessed, that, for his part, he had done nothing but sigh for her ever since she came, and that all the white beauties he had seen never charmed him so absolutely as this fine creature had done, and that no man of any nation ever beheld her that did not fall in love with her, and that she had all the slaves perpetually at her feet, and the whole country resounded with the fame of Clemene, "For so," said he, "we have christened her. But she denies us all with such a noble disdain, that 'tis a miracle to see that she, who can give such eternal desires, should herself be all ice and all unconcerned. She is adorned with the most graceful modesty that ever beautified youth; the softest sigher—that, if she were capable of love, one would swear she languished for some absent, happy man, and so retired, as if she feared a rape even from the god of day, or that the breezes would steal kisses from her delicate mouth. Her task of work some sighing lover every day makes it his petition to perform for her, which she accepts, blushing, and with reluctancy, for fear he will ask her a look for a recompense, which he dares not presume to hope, so great an awe she strikes into the hearts of her admirers."

"I do not wonder," replied the prince, "that Clemene should refuse slaves, being as you say so beautiful, but wonder how she escapes those who can entertain her as you can do; or why, being your slave, you do not oblige her to yield."

"I confess," said Trefry, "when I have, against her will, entertained her with love so long as to be transported with my passion, even above decency, I have been ready to make use of those advantages of strength and force nature has given me. But O, she disarms me with that modesty and weeping so tender and so moving that I retire and thank my stars she overcame me."

The company laughed at his servility to a slave, and Caesar only applauded the nobleness of his passion and nature, since that slave might be noble, or, what was better, have true notions of honour and virtue in her. Thus passed they this night, after having received from the slaves all imaginable respect and obedience. The next day Trefry asked Caesar to walk, when the heat was allayed, and designedly carried him by the cottage of the fair slave, and told him, she whom he spoke of last night lived there retired. "But," says he, "I would not wish you to approach, for I am sure you will be in love as soon as you behold her." Caesar assured him he was proof against all the charms of that sex, and that if he imagined his heart could be so perfidious to love again after Imoinda, he believed he should tear it from his bosom. They had no sooner spoke, but a little shock dog, that Clemene had presented her, which she took great delight in, ran out, and she, not knowing anybody was there, ran to get it in again, and bolted out on those who were just speaking of her, when seeing them, she would have run in again, but Trefry caught her by the hand and cried, "Clemene, however you fly a lover, you ought to pay some respect to this stranger," pointing to Caesar. But she, as if she had resolved never to raise her eyes to the face of a man again, bent 'em the more to the earth when he spoke and gave the prince the leisure to look the more at her. There needed no long gazing or consideration to examine who this fair creature was; he soon saw Imoinda all over her: in a minute he saw her face, her shape, her air, her modesty, and all that called forth his soul with joy at his eyes, and left his body destitute of almost life; it stood without motion and, for a minute, knew not that it had a being, and I believe he had never come to himself, so oppressed he was with overjoy, if he had not met with this allay: that he perceived

Imoinda fall dead in the hands of Trefry. This awakened him, and he ran to her aid, and caught her in his arms, where, by degrees, she came to herself, and 'tis needless to tell with what transports, what ecstasies of joy they both awhile beheld each other without speaking, then snatched each other to their arms, then gaze again, as if they still doubted whether they possessed the blessing they grasped; but when they recovered their speech, 'tis not to be imagined what tender things they expressed to each other, wondering what strange fate had brought 'em again together. They soon informed each other of their fortunes, and equally bewailed their fate, but, at the same time, they mutually protested that even fetters and slavery were soft and easy, and would be supported with joy and pleasure while they could be so happy to possess each other, and to be able to make good their vows. Caesar swore he disdained the empire of the world while he could behold his Imoinda, and she despised grandeur and pomp, those vanities of her sex, when she could gaze on Oroonoko. He adored the very cottage where she resided, and said that little inch of the world would give him more happiness than all the universe could do; and she vowed it was a palace, while adorned with the presence of Oroonoko.

Trefry was infinitely pleased with this novel, and found this Clemene was the fair mistress of whom Caesar had before spoke, and was not a little satisfied that Heaven was so kind to the prince as to sweeten his misfortunes by so lucky an accident; and leaving the lovers to themselves, was impatient to come down to Parham House (which was on the same plantation) to give me an account of what had happened. I was as impatient to make these lovers a visit, having already made a friendship with Caesar, and from his own mouth learned what I have related, which was confirmed by his Frenchman, who was set on shore to seek his fortunes, and of whom they could not make a slave, because a Christian, and he came daily to Parham Hill to see and pay his respects to his pupil prince. So that concerning and interesting myself in all that related to Caesar, whom I had assured of liberty as soon as the governor arrived, I hasted presently to the place where the lovers were, and was infinitely glad to find this beautiful young slave (who had already gained all our esteems for her modesty and her extraordinary prettiness) to be the same I had heard Caesar speak so much of. One may imagine then, we paid her a treble respect, and though, from her being carved in fine flowers and birds all over her body, we took her to be of quality before, yet when we knew Clemene was Imoinda we could not enough admire her.

I had forgot to tell you that those who are nobly born of that country are so delicately cut and razed all over the fore part of the trunk of their bodies, that it looks as if it were japanned, the works being raised like highpoint round the edges of the flowers. Some are only carved with a little flower or bird at the sides of the temples, as was Caesar, and those who are so carved over the body resemble our ancient Picts, that are figured in the chronicles, but these carvings are more delicate.

From that happy day, Caesar took Clemene for his wife, to the general joy of all people; and there was as much magnificence as the country would afford at the celebration of this wedding. And in a very short time after, she conceived with child, which made Caesar even adore her, knowing he was the last of his great race. This new accident made him more impatient of liberty, and he was every day treating with Trefry for his and Clemene's liberty; and offered either gold, or a vast quantity of slaves, which should be paid before they let him go, provided he could have any security that he should go when his ransom was paid. They fed him from day to day with promises, and delayed him till the lord governor should come, so that he began to suspect them of falsehood, and that they would delay him till the time of his wife's delivery, and make a slave of that too, for all the breed is theirs to whom the parents belong. This thought made him very uneasy, and his sullenness gave them some jealousies of him, so that I was obliged by some persons who feared a mutiny (which is very fatal sometimes in those colonies, that abound so with slaves that they exceed the whites in vast numbers) to discourse with Caesar, and to give him all the satisfaction I possibly could; they knew he and Clemene were scarce an hour in a day from my lodgings, that they eat with me, and that I obliged 'em in all things I was capable of. I entertained him with the lives of the Romans and great men, which charmed him to my company; and her, with teaching her all the pretty works that I was mistress of, and telling her stories of nuns, and endeavouring to bring her to the knowledge of the true God. But of all the discourses Caesar liked that the worst, and would never be reconciled to our notions of the Trinity, of which he ever made a jest; it was a riddle, he said, would turn his brain to conceive, and one could not make him understand what faith was. However, these conversations failed not altogether so well to divert him, that he liked the company of us women much above the men, for he could not drink, and he is but an ill companion in that country that cannot. So that obliging him to love us very well, we had all the liberty of speech with him, especially myself, whom he called his great mistress; and indeed my word would go a great way with him. For these reasons, I had opportunity to take notice to him that he was not well pleased of late as he used to be, was more retired and thoughtful, and told him, I took it ill he should suspect we would break our words with him, and not permit both him and Clemene to return to his own kingdom, which was not so long a way; but when he was once on his voyage, he would quickly arrive there. He made me some answers that showed a doubt in him, which made me ask him what advantage it would be to doubt. It would but give us a fear of him, and possibly compel us to treat him so, as I should be very loath to behold; that is, it might occasion his confinement. Perhaps this was not so luckily spoke of me, for I perceived he resented that word which I strove to soften again in vain. However, he assured me that whatsoever resolutions he should take, he would act nothing upon the white people; and as for myself, and those upon that plantation where he was, he would sooner forfeit his eternal liberty, and life itself, than lift his hand against his greatest enemy on that place. He besought me to suffer no fears upon his account, for he could do nothing that honour should not dictate; but he accused himself for having suffered slavery so long. Yet he charged that weakness on love alone, who was capable of making him neglect even glory itself, and for which now he reproaches himself every moment of the day. Much more to this effect he spoke, with an air impatient enough to make me know he would not be long in bondage; and though he suffered only the name of a slave, and had nothing of the toil and labour of one, yet that was sufficient to render him uneasy, and he had been too long idle, who used to be always in action, and in arms. He had a spirit all rough and fierce, and that could not be tamed to lazy rest; and though all endeavours were used to exercise himself in such actions and sports as this world afforded, as running, wrestling, pitching the bar, hunting and fishing, chasing and killing tigers of a monstrous size, which this continent affords in abundance, and wonderful snakes such as Alexander is reported to have encountered at the river of Amazons, and which Caesar took great delight to overcome, yet these were not actions great enough for his large soul, which was still panting after more renowned action.

Before I parted that day with him I got, with much ado, a promise from him to rest yet a little longer with patience, and wait the coming of the lord governor, who was every day expected on our shore. He assured me he would, and this promise he desired me to know was given perfectly in complaisance to me, in whom he had an entire confidence. After this, I neither thought it convenient to trust him much out of our view, nor did the country, who feared him; but with one accord it was advised to treat him fairly and oblige him to remain within such a compass, and that he should be permitted as seldom as could be to go up to the plantations of the Negroes, or, if he did, to be accompanied by some that should be rather in appearance attendants than spies. This care was for some time taken, and Caesar looked upon it as a mark of extraordinary respect, and was glad his discontent had obliged 'em to be more observant to him. He received new assurance from the overseer, which was confirmed to him by the opinion of all the gentlemen of the country, who made their court to him. During this time that we had his company more frequently than hitherto we had had, it may not be unpleasant to relate to you the diversions we entertained him with, or rather he us.

My stay was to be short in that country, because my father died at sea and never arrived to possess the honour was designed him (which was lieutenant general of six and thirty islands, besides the continent of Surinam), nor the advantages he hoped to reap by them, so that though we were obliged to continue on our voyage, we did not intend to stay upon the place. Though, in a word, I must say thus much of it, that certainly had his late Majesty of sacred memory but seen and known what a vast and charming world he had been master of in that continent, he would never have parted so easily with it to the Dutch. 'Tis a continent whose vast extent was never yet known, and may contain more noble earth than all the universe besides, for they say it reaches from East to West one way as far as China, and another to Peru. It affords all things both for beauty and use; 'tis there eternal spring, always the very months of April, May and June; the shades are perpetual, the trees bearing at once all degrees of leaves and fruit, from blooming buds to ripe autumn; groves of oranges, lemons, citrons, figs, nutmegs, and noble aromatics, continually bearing their fragrancies. The trees appearing all like nosegays adorned with flowers of different kind; some are all white, some purple, some scarlet, some blue, some yellow; bearing at the same time ripe fruit and blooming young, or producing every day new. The very wood of all these trees have an intrinsic value above common timber; for they are, when cut, of different colours, glorious to behold, and bear a price considerable to inlay withal. Besides this, they yield rich balm and gums, so that we make our candles of such an aromatic substance as does not only give a sufficient light, but, as they burn, they cast their perfumes all about. Cedar is the common firing, and all the houses are built with it. The very meat we eat, when set on the table, if it be native, I mean of the country, perfumes the whole room, especially a little beast called an armadilly, a thing which I can liken to nothing so well as a rhinoceros; 'tis all in white armour so jointed that it moves as well in it as if it had nothing on. This beast is about the bigness of a pig of six weeks old. But it were endless to give an account of all the diverse wonderful and strange things that country affords, and which we took a very great delight to go in search of, though those adventures are often times fatal and at least dangerous. But while we had Caesar in our company on these designs we feared no harm, nor suffered any.

As soon as I came into the country, the best house in it was presented me, called St John's Hill. It stood on a vast rock of white marble, at the foot of which the river ran a vast depth down, and not to be descended on that side; the little waves, still dashing and washing the foot of this rock, made the softest murmurs and purlings in the world, and the opposite bank was adorned with such vast quantities of different flowers eternally blowing, and every day and hour new, fenced behind 'em with lofty trees of a thousand rare forms and colours, that the prospect was the most raving that sands can create. On the edge of this white rock, towards the river, was a walk or grove of orange and lemon trees, about half the length of the Marl here, whose flowery and fruity bare branches meet at the top, and hindered the sun, whose rays are very fierce there, from entering a beam into the grove; and the cool air that came from the river made it not only fit to entertain people in at all the hottest hours of the day, but refreshed the sweet blossoms and made it always sweet and charming; and sure the whole globe of the world cannot show so delightful a place as this grove was. Not all the gardens of boasted Italy can produce a shade to outvie this, which nature had joined with art to render so exceeding fine, and 'tis a marvel to see how such vast trees, as big as English oaks, could take footing on so solid a rock, and in so little earth as covered that rock, but all things by nature there are rare, delightful and wonderful. But to our sports.

Sometimes we would go surprising and in search of young tigers in their dens, watching when the old ones went forth to forage for prey; and oftentimes we have been in great danger and have fled apace for our lives, when surprised by the dams. But once above all other times we went on this design, and Caesar was with us, who had no sooner stolen a young tiger from her nest but, going off, we encountered the dam bearing a buttock of a cow, which he had torn off with his mighty paw, and going with it towards his den; we had only four women, Caesar, and an English gentleman, brother to Harry Martin, the great Oliverian; we found there was no escaping this enraged and ravenous beast. However, we women fled as fast as we could from it, but our heels had not saved our lives if Caesar had not laid down his cub, when he found the tiger quit her prey to make the more speed towards him, and taking Mr Martin's sword, desired him to stand aside, or follow the ladies. He obeyed him, and Caesar met this monstrous beast of might, size, and vast limbs, who came with open jaws upon him, and fixing his aweful stern eyes full upon those of the beast, and putting himself into a very steady and good aiming posture of defence, ran his sword quite through his breast down to his very heart, home to the hilt of the sword; the dying beast stretched forth her paw and going to grasp his thigh, surprised with death in that very moment, did him no other harm than fixing her long nails in his flesh very deep, feebly wounded him but could not grasp the flesh to tear off any. When he had done this, he holloed to us to return, which after some assurance of his victory we did, and found him lugging out the sword from the bosom of the tiger, who was laid in her blood on the ground. He took up the cub and, with an unconcern that had nothing of the joy or gladness of a victory, he came and laid the whelp at my feet. We all extremely wondered at his daring and at the bigness of the beast, which was about the height of an heifer, but of mighty, great, and strong limbs.

Another time, being in the woods, he killed a tiger which had long infested that part, and borne away abundance of sheep and oxen and other things that were for the support of those to whom they belonged. Abundance of people assailed this beast, some affirming they had shot her with several bullets quite through the body at several times, and some swearing they shot her through the very heart, and they believed she was a devil rather than a mortal thing. Caesar had often said he had a mind to encounter this monster, and spoke with several gentlemen who had attempted her; one crying, "I shot her with so many poisoned arrows," another with his gun in this part of her, and another in that; so that he, remarking all these places where she was shot, fancied still he should overcome her, by giving her another sort of a wound than any had yet done, and one day said (at the table), "What trophies and garlands, ladies, will you make me if I bring you home the heart of this ravenous beast that eats up all your lambs and pigs?" We all promised he should be rewarded at all our hands. So taking a bow, which he choosed out of a great many, he went up in the wood with two gentlemen, where he imagined this devourer to be. They had not passed very far in it but they heard her voice growling and grumbling as if she were pleased with something she was doing. When they came in view, they found her muzzling in the belly of a new-ravished sheep, which she had torn open, and seeing herself approached, she took fast hold of her prey with her forepaws, and set a very fierce raging look on Caesar, without offering to approach him for fear, at the same time, of losing what she had in possession. So that Caesar remained a good while only taking aim and getting an opportunity to shoot her when he designed. 'Twas some time before he could accomplish it, and to wound her and not kill her would but have enraged her more and endangered him. He had a quiver of arrows at his side, so that if one failed he could be supplied; at last, retiring a little, he gave her opportunity to eat, for he found she was ravenous, and fell to as soon as she saw him retire, being more eager of her prey than of doing new mischiefs. When he, going softly to one side of her, and hiding his person behind certain herbage that grew high and thick, he took so good aim that, as he intended, he shot her just into the eye, and the arrow was sent with so good a will, and so sure a hand, that it stuck in her brain, and made her caper, and become mad for a moment or two, but being seconded by another arrow, he fell dead upon the prey.

Caesar cut him open with a knife to see where those wounds were that had been reported to him, and why he did not die of 'em. But I shall now relate a thing that possibly will find no credit among men, because 'tis a notion commonly received with us, that nothing can receive a wound in the heart and live; but when the heart of this courageous animal was taken out, there were seven bullets of lead in it, and the wounds seamed up with great scars, and she lived with the bullets a great while, for it was long since they were shot. This heart the conqueror brought up to us, and 'twas a very great curiosity, which all the country came to see, and which gave Caesar occasion of many fine discourses of accidents in war and strange escapes.

At other times he would go a-fishing and discoursing on that diversion, he found we had in that country a very strange fish, called a numb-eel (an eel of which I have eaten), that while it is alive, it has a quality so cold that those who are angling, though with a line of never so great a length with a rod at the end of it, it shall, in the same minute the bait is touched by this eel, seize him or her that holds the rod with benumbedness, that shall deprive 'em of sense for a while; and some have fallen into the water, and others dropped as dead on the banks of the rivers where they stood, as soon as this fish touches the bait. Caesar used to laugh at this, and believed it impossible a man could lose his force at the touch of a fish, and could not understand that philosophy, that a cold quality should be of that nature. However, he had a great curiosity to try whether it would have the same effect on him it had on others, and often tried, but in vain. At last the sought-for fish came to the bait as he stood angling on the bank, and instead of throwing away the rod, or giving it a sudden twitch out of the water, whereby he might have caught both the eel and have dismissed the rod, before it could have too much power over him, for experiment's sake he grasped it but the harder, and fainting fell into the river, and being still possessed of the rod, the tide carried him senseless as he was a great way till an Indian boat took him up and perceived, when they touched him, a numbness seize them, and by that knew the rod was in his hand, which, with a paddle (that is, a short oar) they struck away and snatched it into the boat, eel and all. If Caesar were almost dead with the effect of this fish, he was more so with that of the water, where he had remained the space of going a league, and they found they had much ado to bring him back to life. But, at last, they did, and brought him home, where he was in a few hours well recovered and refreshed, and not a little ashamed to find he should be overcome by an eel, and that all the people who heard his defiance would laugh at him. But we cheered him up, and he, being convinced, we had the eel at supper, which was a quarter of an eel about, and most delicate meat, and was of the more value since it cost so dear as almost the life of so gallant a man.

About this time we were in many mortal fears about some disputes the English had with the Indians, so that we could scarce trust ourselves without great numbers to go to any Indian towns or place where they abode, for fear they should fall upon us, as they did immediately after my coming away, and that it was in the possession of the Dutch, who used 'em not so civilly as the English, so that they cut in pieces all they could take, getting into houses and hanging up the mother and all her children about her; and cut a footman I left behind me all in joints, and nailed him to trees.

This feud began while I was there, so that I lost half the satisfaction I proposed in not seeing and visiting the Indian towns. But one day, bemoaning of our misfortunes upon this account, Caesar told us we need not fear, for if we had a mind to go, he would undertake to be our guard. Some would, but most would not venture; about eighteen of us resolved and took barge, and, after eight days, arrived near an Indian town, but approaching it, the hearts of some of our company failed, and they would not venture on shore, so we polled who would and who would not. For my part, I said if Caesar would, I would go. He resolved, so did my brother and my woman, a maid of good courage. Now none of us speaking the language of the people, and imagining we should have a half-diversion in gazing only, and not knowing what they said, we took a fisherman that lived at the mouth of the river who had been a long inhabitant there, and obliged him to go with us. But because he was known to the Indians as trading among 'em, and being by long living there become a perfect Indian in colour, we, who resolved to surprise 'em by making 'em see something they never had seen (that is, white people), resolved only myself, my brother and woman should go; so Caesar, the fisherman and the rest, hiding behind some thick reeds and flowers that grew on the banks, let us pass on towards the town, which was on the bank of the river all along. A little distant from the houses, or huts, we saw some dancing, others busied in fetching and carrying of water from the river; they had no sooner spied us, but they set up a loud cry that frighted us at first. We thought it had been for those that should kill us, but it seems it was of wonder and amazement. They were all naked, and we were dressed so as is most commode for the hot countries, very glittering and rich, so that we appeared extremely fine. My own hair was cut short, and I had a taffety cap, with black feathers on my head. My brother was in a stuff suit, with silver loops and buttons, and abundance of green ribbon. This was all infinitely surprising to them, and because we saw them stand still till we approached 'em, we took heart and advanced, came up to 'em, and offered 'em our hands, which they took and looked on us round about, calling still for more company, who came swarming out, all wondering and crying out: "Tepeeme," taking their hair up in their hands and spreading it wide to those they called out to, as if they would say (as indeed it signified) "numberless wonders," or not to be recounted, no more than to number the hair of their heads. By degrees they grew more bold, and from gazing upon us round, they touched us, laying their hands upon all the features of our faces, feeling our breasts and arms, taking up one petticoat, then wondering to see another; admiring our shoes and stockings, but more our garters, which we gave 'em, and they tied about their legs, being laced with silver lace at the ends, for they much esteem any shining things. In fine, we suffered 'em to survey us as they pleased, and we thought they would never have done admiring us. When Caesar and the rest saw we were received with such wonder, they came up to us, and finding the Indian trader whom they knew (for 'tis by these fishermen, called Indian traders, we hold a commerce with 'em, for they love not to go far from home, and we never go to them), when they saw him, therefore, they set up a new joy, and cried, in their language, "Oh, here's our Tiguamy, and we shall now know whether those things can speak." So, advancing to him, some of 'em gave him their hands and cried, "Amora, Tiguamy"— which is as much as, "How do you" or "Welcome friend;" and all, with one din, began to gabble to him and asked if we had sense and wit, if we could talk of affairs of life and war, as they could do, if we could hunt, swim, and do a thousand things they use. He answered 'em we could. Then they invited us into their houses, and dressed venison and buffalo for us, and, going out, gathered a leaf of a tree called a sarumbo leaf, of six yards long, and spread it on the ground for a tablecloth, and cutting another in pieces instead of plates, setting us on little low Indian stools, which they cut out of one entire piece of wood and paint in a sort of japan work, they serve everyone their mess on these pieces of leaves, and it was very good, but too high seasoned with pepper. When we had eat, my brother and I took out our flutes, and played to 'em, which gave 'em new wonder, and I soon perceived, by an admiration that is natural to these people, and by the extreme ignorance and simplicity of 'em, it were not difficult to establish any unknown or extravagant religion among them, and to impose any notions or fictions upon 'em. For seeing a kinsman of mine set some paper afire with a burning glass, a trick they had never before seen, they were like to have adored him for a god, and begged he would give them the characters or figures of his name, that they might oppose it against winds and storms, which he did, and they held it up in those seasons, and fancied it had a charm to conquer them, and kept it like a holy relic. They are very superstitious, and called him the Great Peeie; that is, prophet. They showed us their Indian Peeie, a youth of about sixteen years old, as handsome as nature could make a man. They consecrate a beautiful youth from his infancy, and all arts are used to complete him in the finest manner, both in beauty and shape. He is bred to all the little arts and cunning they are capable of, to all the legerdemain, tricks, and sleight of hand, whereby he imposes upon the rabble, and is both a doctor in physic and divinity, and by these tricks makes the sick believe he sometimes eases their pains by drawing from the afflicted part little serpents, or odd flies, or worms, or any strange thing, and though they have besides undoubted good remedies for almost all their diseases, they cure the patient more by fancy than by medicines, and make themselves feared, loved, and reverenced. This young Peeie had a very young wife, who seeing my brother kiss her, came running and kissed me; after this, they kissed one another, and made it a very great jest, it being so novel, and new admiration and laughing went round the multitude, that they never will forget that ceremony never before used or known. Caesar had a mind to see and talk with their war captains, and we were conducted to one of their houses, where we beheld several of the great captains, who had been at council. But so frightful a vision it was to see 'em no fancy can create, no such dreams can represent so dreadful a spectacle. For my part, I took 'em for hobgoblins, or fiends, rather than men; but however their shapes appeared, their souls were very humane and noble, but some wanted their noses, some their lips, some both noses and lips, some their ears, and others cut through each cheek with long slashes through which their teeth appeared. They had other several formidable wounds and scars, or rather dismemberings; they had Comitias, or little aprons before 'em, and girdles of cotton, with their knives naked stuck in it, a bow at their backs and a quiver of arrows on their thighs, and most had feathers on their heads of diverse colours. They cried, "Amora Tiguamy" to us at our entrance, and were pleased we said as much to 'em; they seated us and gave us drink of the best sort, and wondered, as much as the others had done before, to see us. Caesar was marvelling as much at their faces, wondering how they should all be so wounded in war; he was impatient to know how they all came by those frightful marks of rage or malice, rather than wounds got in noble battle. They told us, by our interpreter, that when any war was waging, two men chosen out by some old captain, whose fighting was past, and who could only teach the theory of war, these two men were to stand in competition for the generalship, or great war captain, and being brought before the old judges, now past labour, they are asked what they dare do to show they are worthy to lead an army. When he who is first asked, making no reply, cuts off his nose and throws it contemptibly on the ground, and the other does something to himself that he thinks surpasses him, and perhaps deprives himself of lips and an eye. So they slash on till one gives out, and many have died in this debate. And 'tis by a passive valour they show and prove their activity: a sort of courage too brutal to be applauded by our black hero, nevertheless he expressed his esteem of 'em.

In this voyage Caesar begot so good an understanding between the Indians and the English, that there were no more fears or heartburnings during our stay, but we had a perfect, open, and free trade with 'em. Many things remarkable and worthy reciting we met with in this short voyage, because Caesar made it his business to search out and provide for our entertainment, especially to please his dearly adored Imoinda, who was a sharer in all our adventures, we being resolved to make her chains as easy as we could, and to compliment the prince in that manner that most obliged him.

As we were coming up again, we met with some Indians of strange aspects; that is, of a larger size, and other sort of features than those of our country. Our Indian slaves that rowed us asked 'em some questions, but they could not understand us, but showed us a long cotton string with several knots on it, and told us they had been coming from the mountains so many moons as there were knots. They were habited in skins of a strange beast and brought along with 'em bags of gold dust which, as well as they could give us to understand, came streaming in little small channels down the high mountains when the rains fell, and offered to be the convoy to any body or persons that would go to the mountains. We carried these men up to Parham, where they were kept till the lord governor came, and because all the country was mad to be going on this golden adventure, the governor, by his letters, commanded (for they sent some of the gold to him) that a guard should be set at the mouth of the river of Amazons (a river so called, almost as broad as the river of Thames), and prohibited all people from going up that river, it conducting to those mountains of gold. But we going off for England before the project was further prosecuted, and the governor being drowned in a hurricane, either the design died, or the Dutch have the advantage of it, and 'tis to be bemoaned what His Majesty lost by losing that part of America.

Though this digression is a little from my story, however, since it contains some proofs of the curiosity and daring of this great man, I was content to omit nothing of his character.

It was thus for some time we diverted him, but now Imoinda began to show she was with child, and did nothing but sigh and weep for the captivity of her lord, herself and the infant yet unborn, and believed, if it were so hard to gain the liberty of two, 'twould be more difficult to get that for three. Her griefs were so many darts in the great heart of Caesar, and taking his opportunity one Sunday, when all the whites were overtaken in drink, as there were abundance of several trades and slaves for four years that inhabited among the Negro houses, and Sunday was their day of debauch (otherwise they were a sort of spies upon Caesar), he went pretending out of goodness to 'em to feast amongst 'em, and sent all his music and ordered a great treat for the whole gang, about three hundred Negroes, and about a hundred and fifty were able to bear arms, such as they had, which were sufficient to do execution with spirits accordingly, for the English had none but rusty swords, that no strength could draw from a scabbard, except the people of particular quality, who took care to oil 'em and keep 'em in good order. The guns also, unless here and there one, or those newly carried from England, would do no good or harm, for 'tis the nature of that country to rust and eat up iron, or any metals but gold and silver. And they are very unexpert at the bow, which the Negroes and Indians are perfect masters of.

Caesar, having singled out these men from the women and children, made an harangue to 'em of the miseries and ignominies of slavery, counting up all their toils and sufferings under such loads, burdens, and drudgeries as were fitter for beasts than men, senseless brutes than human souls. He told 'em it was not for days, months or years, but for eternity; there was no end to be of their misfortunes. They suffered not like men who might find a glory and fortitude in oppression, but like dogs that loved the whip and bell and fawned the more they were beaten; that they had lost the divine quality of men, and were become insensible asses, fit only to bear; nay worse, an ass, or dog, or horse, having done his duty, could lie down in retreat, and rise to work again, and while he did his duty, endured no stripes, but men, villainous, senseless men such as they, toiled on all the tedious week till black Friday, and then whether they worked or not, whether they were faulty or meriting, they promiscuously, the innocent with the guilty, suffered the infamous whip, the sordid stripes from their fellow slaves till their blood trickled from all parts of their body, blood whose every drop ought to be revenged with a life of some of those tyrants that impose it.

"And why," said he, "my dear friends and fellow sufferers, should we be slaves to an unknown people? Have they vanquished us nobly in fight? Have they won us in honourable battle? And are we by the chance of war become their slaves? This would not anger a noble heart, this would not animate a soldier's soul; no, but we are bought and sold like apes or monkeys, to be the sport of women, fools, and cowards, and the support of rogues, runagates, that have abandoned their own countries for rapine, murders, thefts, and villainies. Do you not hear every day how they upbraid each other with infamy of life, below the wildest salvages, and shall we render obedience to such a degenerate race, who have no one humane virtue left to distinguish 'em from the vilest creatures? Will you, I say, suffer the lash from such hands?"

They all replied, with one accord, "No, no, no! Caesar has spoke like a great captain, like a great king."

After this he would have proceeded, but was interrupted by a tall Negro of some more quality than the rest. His name was Tuscan, who, bowing at the feet of Caesar, cried: "My Lord, we have listened with joy and attention to what you have said, and, were we only men, would follow so great a leader through the world. But O, consider, we are husbands and parents too, and have things more dear to us than life: our wives and children, unfit for travel in these unpassable woods, mountains and bogs; we have not only difficult lands to overcome, but rivers to wade and monsters to encounter, ravenous beasts of prey—" To this, Caesar replied that honour was the first principle in nature that was to be obeyed; that as no man would pretend to that without all the acts of virtue, compassion, charity, love, justice, and reason, he found it not inconsistent with that to take an equal care of their wives and children, as they would of themselves, and that he did not design, when he led them to freedom and glorious liberty, that they should leave that better part of themselves to perish by the hand of the tyrant's whip. But if there were a woman among them so degenerate from love and virtue to choose slavery before the pursuit of her husband, and with the hazard of her life, to share with him in his fortunes, that such an one ought to be abandoned and left as a prey to the common enemy.

To which they all agreed—and bowed. After this, he spoke of the impassable woods and rivers, and convinced 'em, the more danger, the more glory. He told them that he had heard of one Hannibal, a great captain, had cut his way through mountains of solid rocks, and should a few shrubs oppose them, which they could fire before 'em? No, 'twas a trifling excuse to men resolved to die, or overcome. As for bogs, they are with a little labour filled and hardened, and the rivers could be no obstacle, since they swam by nature, at least by custom, from their first hour of their birth; that when the children were weary they must carry them by turns, and the woods and their own industry would afford them food. To this they all assented with joy.

Tuscan then demanded what he would do. He said, they would travel towards the sea, plant a new colony, and defend it by their valour, and when they could find a ship, either driven by stress of weather or guided by providence that way, they would seize it and make it a prize, till it had transported them to their own countries; at least, they should be made free in his kingdom, and be esteemed as his fellow sufferers, and men that had the courage and the bravery to attempt, at least, for liberty, and if they died in the attempt, it would be more brave than to live in perpetual slavery.

They bowed and kissed his feet at this resolution, and with one accord vowed to follow him to death. And that night was appointed to begin their march. They made it known to their wives and directed them to tie their hamaca about their shoulder, and under their arm like a scarf, and to lead their children that could go, and carry those that could not. The wives, who pay an entire obedience to their husbands, obeyed, and stayed for 'em where they were appointed. The men stayed but to furnish themselves with what defensive arms they could get, and all met at the rendezvous, where Caesar made a new encouraging speech to 'em, and led 'em out.

But, as they could not march far that night, on Monday early, when the overseers went to call 'em all together to go to work, they were extremely surprised to find not one upon the place, but all fled with what baggage they had. You may imagine this news was not only suddenly spread all over the plantation, but soon reached the neighbouring ones, and we had by noon about six hundred men, they call the militia of the country, that came to assist us in the pursuit of the fugitives. But never did one see so comical an army march forth to war. The men, of any fashion, would not concern themselves, though it were almost the common cause, for such revoltings are very ill examples, and have very fatal consequences oftentimes in many colonies. But they had a respect for Caesar, and all hands were against the Parhamites, as they called those of Parham Plantation, because they did not, in the first place, love the lord governor, and secondly, they would have it that Caesar was ill-used and baffled with; and 'tis not impossible but some of the best in the country was of his council in this flight, and depriving us of all the slaves, so that they of the better sort would not meddle in the matter. The deputy governor, of whom I have had no great occasion to speak, and who was the most fawning, fair-tongued fellow in the world, and one that pretended the most friendship to Caesar, was now the only violent man against him, and though he had nothing, and so need fear nothing, yet talked and looked bigger than any man. He was a fellow whose character is not fit to be mentioned with the worst of the slaves. This fellow would lead his army forth to meet Caesar, or rather, to pursue him; most of their arms were of those sort of cruel whips they call cat-with-nine-tails; some had rusty, useless guns for show, others old basket-hilts whose blades had never seen the light in this age, and others had long staffs and clubs. Mr Trefry went along, rather to be a mediator than a conqueror in such a battle, for he foresaw, and knew, if by fighting they put the Negroes into despair, they were a sort of sullen fellows, that would drown or kill themselves before they would yield, and he advised that fair means was best. But Byam was one that abounded in his own wit, and would take his own measures. It was not hard to find these fugitives, for as they fled they were forced to fire and cut the woods before 'em, so that night or day they pursued 'em by the light they made, and by the path they had cleared. But as soon as Caesar found he was pursued, he put himself in a posture of defence, placing all the women and children in the rear, and himself, with Tuscan by his side, or next to him, all promising to die or conquer. Encouraged thus, they never stood to parley, but fell on pellmell upon the English and killed some, and wounded a good many, they having recourse to their whips as the best of the weapons. And as they observed no order, they perplexed the enemy so sorely, with lashing 'em in the eyes, and the women and children seeing their husbands so treated, being of fearful, cowardly dispositions, and hearing the English cry out, "Yield and live; yield and be pardoned!," they all run in amongst their husbands and fathers, and hung about 'em, crying out, "Yield, yield, and leave Caesar to their revenge," that by degrees the slaves abandoned Caesar and left him only Tuscan and his heroic Imoinda, who grown big as she was, did nevertheless press near her lord, having a bow and a quiver full of poisoned arrows, which she managed with such dexterity that she wounded several, and shot the governor into the shoulder, of which wound he had like to have died, but that an Indian woman, his mistress, sucked the wound, and cleansed it from the venom. But however, he stirred not from the place till he had parleyed with Caesar, who he found was resolved to die fighting, and would not be taken; no more would Tuscan or Imoinda. But he, more thirsting after revenge of another sort than that of depriving him of life, now made use of all his art of talking and dissembling, and besought Caesar to yield himself upon terms which he himself should propose, and should be sacredly assented to and kept by him. He told him, it was not that he any longer feared him, or could believe the force of two men, and a young heroine, could overcome all them, with all the slaves now on their side also, but it was the vast esteem he had for his person, the desire he had to serve so gallant a man, and to hinder himself from the reproach hereafter of having been the occasion of the death of a prince whose valour and magnanimity deserved the empire of the world. He protested to him, he looked upon this action as gallant and brave, however tending to the prejudice of his lord and master who would, by it, have lost so considerable a number of slaves; that this flight of his should be looked on as a heat of youth and rashness of a too-forward courage, and an unconsidered impatience of liberty, and no more, and that he laboured in vain to accomplish that which they would effectually perform as soon as any ship arrived that would touch on his coast.

"So that if you will be pleased," continued he, "to surrender yourself, all imaginable respect shall be paid you, and yourself, your wife, and child, if it be here born, shall depart free out of our land." But Caesar would hear of no composition, though Byam urged, if he pursued and went on in his design, he would inevitably perish, either by great snakes, wild beasts, or hunger, and he ought to have regard to his wife, whose condition required ease and not the fatigues of tedious travel, where she could not be secured from being devoured. But Caesar told him, there was no faith in the white men or the gods they adored, who instructed 'em in principles so false that honest men could not live amongst 'em; though no people professed so much, none performed so little; that he knew what he had to do when he dealt with men of honour, but with them a man ought to be eternally on his guard, and never to eat and drink with Christians without his weapon of defence in his hand, and for his own security never to credit one word they spoke. As for the rashness and inconsiderateness of his action, he would confess the governor is in the right, and that he was ashamed of what he had done, in endeavouring to make those free who were by nature slaves, poor, wretched rogues, fit to be used as Christians' tools, dogs treacherous and cowardly fit for such masters, and they wanted only but to be whipped into the knowledge of the Christian gods to be the vilest of all creeping things, to learn to worship such deities as had not power to make 'em just, brave, or honest. In fine, after a thousand things of this nature, not fit here to be recited, he told Byam he had rather die than live upon the same earth with such dogs.

But Trefry and Byam pleaded and protested together so much, that Trefry, believing the governor to mean what he said, and speaking very cordially himself, generously put himself into Caesar's hands, and took him aside, and persuaded him, even with tears, to live by surrendering himself, and to name his conditions. Caesar was overcome by his wit and reasons, and in consideration of Imoinda, and demanding what he desired, and that it should be ratified by their hands in writing, because he had perceived that was the common way of contract between man and man amongst the whites. All this was performed, and Tuscan's pardon was put in, and they surrender to the governor, who walked peaceably down into the plantation with 'em, after giving order to bury their dead. Caesar was very much toiled with the bustle of the day, for he had fought like a Fury, and what mischief was done, he and Tuscan performed alone, and gave their enemies a fatal proof that they durst do anything, and feared no mortal force.

But they were no sooner arrived at the place where all the slaves receive their punishments of whipping, but they laid hands on Caesar and Tuscan, faint with heat and toil, and, surprising them, bound them to two several stakes, and whipped them in a most deplorable and inhumane manner, rending the very flesh from their bones, especially Caesar, who was not perceived to make any moan, or to alter his face, only to roll his eyes on the faithless governor, and those he believed guilty, with fierceness and indignation; and to complete his rage, he saw every one of those slaves who, but a few days before, adored him as something more than mortal, now had a whip to give him some lashes, while he strove not to break his fetters, though if he had, it were impossible. But he pronounced a woe and revenge from his eyes that darted fire, that 'twas at once both aweful and terrible to behold.

When they thought they were sufficiently revenged on him, they untied him, almost fainting with loss of blood from a thousand wounds all over his body, from which they had rent his clothes, and led him bleeding and naked as he was, and loaded him all over with irons, and then rubbed his wounds, to complete their cruelty, with Indian pepper, which had like to have made him raving mad, and in this condition made him so fast to the ground that he could not stir, if his pains and wounds would have given him leave. They spared Imoinda, and did not let her see this barbarity committed towards her lord, but carried her down to Parham, and shut her up, which was not in kindness to her, but for fear she should die with the sight, or miscarry, and then they should lose a young slave, and perhaps the mother.

You must know, that when the news was brought on Monday morning that Caesar had betaken himself to the woods and carried with him all the Negroes, we were possessed with extreme fear which no persuasions could dissipate that he would secure himself till night, and then, that he would come down and cut all our throats. This apprehension made all the females of us fly down the river to be secured, and while we were away they acted this cruelty. For I suppose I had authority and interest enough there, had I suspected any such thing, to have prevented it, but we had not gone many leagues but the news overtook us that Caesar was taken, and whipped like a common slave. We met on the river with Colonel Martin, a man of great gallantry, wit and goodness, and whom I have celebrated in a character of my new comedy by his own name in memory of so brave a man. He was wise and eloquent, and, from the fineness of his parts, bore a great sway over the hearts of all the colony. He was a friend to Caesar, and resented this false dealing with him very much. We carried him back to Parham thinking to have made an accommodation. When we came, the first news we heard was that the governor was dead of a wound Imoinda had given him, but it was not so well; but it seems he would have the pleasure of beholding the revenge he took on Caesar, and before the cruel ceremony was finished, he dropped down, and then they perceived the wound he had on his shoulder was by a venomed arrow which, as I said, his Indian mistress healed by sucking the wound.

We were no sooner arrived, but we went up to the plantation to see Caesar, whom we found in a very miserable and un-expressible condition, and I have a thousand times admired how he lived in so much tormenting pain. We said all things to him that trouble, pity and good nature could suggest, protesting our innocency of the fact, and our abhorrence of such cruelties, making a thousand professions of services to him, and begging as many pardons for the offenders, till we said so much that he believed we had no hand in his ill treatment, but told us he could never pardon Byam; as for Trefry, he confessed he saw his grief and sorrow for his suffering, which he could not hinder, but was like to have been beaten down by the very slaves for speaking in his defence. But for Byam, who was their leader, their head, and should, by his justice and honour, have been an example to 'em—for him, he wished to live to take a dire revenge of him and said, "It had been well for him if he had sacrificed me instead of giving me the contemptible whip." He refused to talk much, but begging us to give him our hands, he took 'em and protested never to lift up his to do us any harm. He had a great respect for Colonel Martin, and always took his counsel like that of a parent, and assured him he would obey him in anything, but his revenge on Byam.

"Therefore," said he, "for his own safety, let him speedily dispatch me, for if I could dispatch myself, I would not till that justice were done to my injured person and the contempt of a soldier. No, I would not kill myself, even after a whipping, but will be content to live with that infamy, and be pointed at by every grinning slave, till I have completed my revenge, and then you shall see that Oroonoko scorns to live with the indignity that was put on Caesar."

All we could do could get no more words from him, and we took care to have him put immediately into a healing bath to rid him of his pepper, and ordered a chirurgeon to anoint him with healing balm, which he suffered, and in some time he began to be able to walk and eat. We failed not to visit him every day, and to that end had him brought to an apartment at Parham.

The governor was no sooner recovered and had heard of the menaces of Caesar but he called his council who (not to disgrace them, or burlesque the government there) consisted of such notorious villains as Newgate never transported, and possibly originally were such, who understood neither the laws of God or man, and had no sort of principles to make 'em worthy the name of men, but at the very council table would contradict and fight with one another; and swear so bloodily that 'twas terrible to hear and see 'em. (Some of 'em were afterwards hanged when the Dutch took possession of the place; others sent off in chains.) But calling these special rulers of the nation together, and requiring their counsel in this weighty affair, they all concluded that (damn 'em) it might be their own cases, and that Caesar ought to be made an example to all the Negroes to fright 'em from daring to threaten their betters, their lords and masters, and, at this rate, no man was safe from his own slaves and concluded *nemine contradicente* that Caesar should be hanged.

Trefry then thought it time to use his authority, and told Byam his command did not extend to his lord's plantation, and that Parham was as much exempt from the law as Whitehall, and that they ought no more to touch the servants of the lord (who there represented the King's person) than they could those about the King himself, and that Parham was a sanctuary, and though his lord were absent in person, his power was still in being there, which he had entrusted with him, as far as the dominions of his particular plantations reached, and all that belonged to it—the rest of the country, as Byam was lieutenant to his lord, he might exercise his tyranny upon. Trefry had others as powerful, or more, that interested themselves in Caesar's life, and absolutely said he should be defended. So turning the governor and his wise council out of doors (for they sat at Parham House), they set a guard upon our landing place and would admit none but those we called friends to us and Caesar.

The governor, having remained wounded at Parham till his recovery was completed, Caesar did not know but he was still there, and indeed, for the most part, his time was spent there, for he was one that loved to live at other people's expense, and if he were a day absent, he was ten present there, and used to play and walk and hunt and fish with Caesar, so that Caesar did not at all doubt, if he once recovered strength, but he should find an opportunity of being revenged on him, though, after such a revenge, he could not hope to live, for if he escaped the fury of the English mobile, who perhaps would have been glad of the occasion to have killed him, he was resolved not to survive his whipping; yet he had some tender hours a repenting softness, which he called his fits of coward, wherein he struggled with love for the victory of his heart, which took part with his charming Imoinda there. But, for the most part, his time was passed in melancholy thought and black designs; he considered, if he should do this deed and die, either in the attempt or after it, he left his lovely Imoinda a prey or, at best, a slave to the enraged multitude. His great heart could not endure that thought. "Perhaps," said he, "she may be first ravished by every brute, exposed first to their nasty lusts, and then a shameful death." No, he could not live a moment under that apprehension, too insupportable to be borne. These were his thoughts, and his silent arguments with his heart, as he told us afterwards, so that now resolving not only to kill Byam, but all those he thought had enraged him, pleasing his great heart with the fancied slaughter he should make over the whole face of the plantation, he first resolved on a deed that (however horrid it at first appeared to us all) when we had heard his reasons, we thought it brave and just. Being able to walk and, as he believed, fit for the execution of his great design, he begged Trefry to trust him into the air, believing a walk would do him good, which was granted him and, taking Imoinda with him as he used to do in his more happy and calmer days, he led her up into a wood, where, after (with a thousand sighs and long gazing silently on her face, while tears gushed in spite of him from his eyes) he told her his design, first of killing her, and then his enemies, and next himself, and the impossibility of escaping and therefore he told her the necessity of dying. He found the heroic wife faster pleading for death than he was to propose it, when she found his fixed resolution, and on her knees besought him not to leave her a prey to his enemies. He, grieved to death, yet pleased at her noble resolution, took her up and embracing her with all the passion and languishment of a dying lover, drew his knife to kill this treasure of his soul, this pleasure of his eyes; while tears trickled down his cheeks, hers were smiling with joy she should die by so noble a hand, and be sent in her own country (for that's their notion of the next world) by him she so tenderly loved and so truly adored in this, for wives have a respect for their husbands equal to what any other people pay a deity, and when a man finds any occasion to quit his wife, if he love her, she dies by his hand, if not, he sells her or suffers some other to kill her. It being thus, you may believe the deed was soon resolved on, and 'tis not to be doubted, but the parting, the eternal leave-taking of two such lovers, so greatly born, so sensible, so beautiful, so young, and so fond, must be very moving, as the relation of it was to me afterwards.

All that love could say in such cases being ended, and all the intermitting irresolutions being adjusted, the lovely, young and adored victim lays herself down before the sacrificer, while he, with a hand resolved, and a heart breaking within, gave the fatal stroke; first cutting her throat, and then severing her yet smiling face from that delicate body, pregnant as it was with the fruits of tenderest love. As soon as he had done, he laid the body decently on leaves and flowers, of which he made a bed and concealed it under the same coverlid of nature; only her face he left yet bare to look on, but when he found she was dead and passed all retrieve, never more to bless him with her eyes and soft language, his grief swelled up to rage, he tore, he raved, he roared like some monster of the wood, calling on the loved name of Imoinda; a thousand times he turned the fatal knife that did the deed toward his own heart, with a resolution to go immediately after her, but dire revenge, which now was a thousand times more fierce in his soul than before, prevents him, and he would cry out, "No, since I have sacrificed Imoinda to my revenge, shall I lose that glory which I have purchased so dear as at the price of the fairest, dearest, softest creature that ever nature made? No, no!." Then, at her name, grief would get the ascendant of rage, and he would lie down by her side, and water her face with showers of tears, which never were wont to fall from those eyes, and however bent he was on his intended slaughter, he had not power to stir from the sight of this dear object, now more beloved and more adored than ever.

He remained in this deploring condition for two days, and never rose from the ground where he had made his sad sacrifice; at last, rousing from her side, and accusing himself with living too long now Imoinda was dead, and that the deaths of those barbarous enemies were deferred too long, he resolved now to finish the great work. But, offering to rise, he found his strength so decayed that he reeled to and fro like boughs assailed by contrary winds, so that he was forced to lie down again, and try to summon all his courage to his aid. He found his brains turn round and his eyes were dizzy, and objects appeared not the same to him they were wont to do; his breath was short, and all his limbs surprised with a faintness he had never felt before. He had not eat in two days, which was one occasion of this feebleness, but excess of grief was the greatest; yet still he hoped he should recover vigour to act his design, and lay expecting it yet six days longer, still mourning over the dead idol of his heart, and striving every day to rise, but could not.

In all this time you may believe we were in no little affliction for Caesar and his wife; some were of opinion he was escaped never to return, others thought some accident had happened to him. But however, we failed not to send out an hundred people several ways to search for him; a party of about forty went that way he took, among whom was Tuscan, who was perfectly reconciled to Byam. They had not gone very far into the wood, but they smelt an unusual smell, as of a dead body, for stinks must be very noisome that can be distinguished among such a quantity of natural sweets as every inch of that land produces. So that they concluded they should find him dead, or somebody that was so; they passed on towards it, as loathsome as it was, and made such a rustling among the leaves that lie thick on the ground by continual falling, that

Caesar heard he was approached, and though he had, during the space of these eight days endeavoured to rise, but found he wanted strength, yet looking up and seeing his pursuers, he rose and reeled to a neighbouring tree, against which he fixed his back, and being within a dozen yards of those that advanced and saw him, he called out to them, and bid them approach no nearer if they would be safe, so that they stood still and hardly believing their eyes, that would persuade them that it was Caesar that spoke to 'em, so much was he altered. They asked him what he had done with his wife, for they smelt a stink that almost struck them dead. He, pointing to the dead body, sighing, cried: "Behold her there." They put off the flowers that covered her with their sticks and found she was killed, and cried out, "Oh monster that hast murdered thy wife." Then asking him why he did so cruel a deed, he replied he had no leisure to answer impertinent questions. "You may go back," continued he, "and tell the faithless governor he may thank fortune that I am breathing my last, and that my arm is too feeble to obey my heart in what it had designed him." But his tongue faltering and trembling, he could scarce end what he was saying.

The English, taking advantage by his weakness, cried, "Let us take him alive by all means." He heard 'em, and as if he had revived from a fainting, or a dream, he cried out, "No Gentlemen, you are deceived, you will find no more Caesars to be whipped, no more find a faith in me. Feeble as you think me, I have strength yet left to secure me from a second indignity." They swore all anew, and he only shook his head and beheld them with scorn. Then they cried out, "Who will venture on this single man? Will nobody?"

They stood all silent while Caesar replied, "Fatal will be the attempt to the first adventurer, let him assure himself," and at that word held up his knife in a menacing posture. "Look ye, ye faithless crew," said he, "'Tis not life I seek, nor am I afraid of dying," and at that word cut a piece of flesh from his own throat and threw it at 'em, "yet still I would live if I could till I had perfected my revenge. But oh it cannot be, I feel life gliding from my eyes and heart, and if I make not haste, I shall yet fall a victim to the shameful whip." At that he ripped up his own belly, and took his bowels and pulled 'em out with what strength he could, while some, on their knees imploring, besought him to hold his hand. But when they saw him tottering, they cried out, "Will none venture on him?" A bold English cried, "Yes, if he were the devil" (taking courage when he saw him almost dead) and swearing a horrid oath for his farewell to the world, he rushed on Caesar [who] with his armed hand met him so fairly as stuck him to the heart and he fell dead at his feet.

Tuscan, seeing that, cried out, "I love thee, O Caesar, and therefore will not let thee die if possible" and, running to him, took him in his arms, but, at the same time, warding a blow that Caesar made at his bosom, he received it quite through his arm, and Caesar, having not the strength to pluck the knife forth, though he attempted it, Tuscan neither pulled it out himself, nor suffered it to be pulled out, but came down with it sticking in his arm, and the reason he gave for it was, because the air should not get into the wound. They put their hands across and carried Caesar between six of 'em, fainted as he was, and they thought dead, or just dying, and they brought him to Parham, and laid him on a couch, and had the chirurgeon immediately to him, who dressed his wounds and sewed up his belly and used means to bring him to life, which they effected. We ran all to see him, and, if before we thought him so beautiful a sight, he was now so altered that his face was like a death's head blacked over, nothing but teeth and eyeholes. For some days we suffered nobody to speak to him, but caused cordials to be poured down his throat, which sustained his life, and in six or seven days he recovered his senses, for you must know that wounds are almost to a miracle cured in the Indies, unless wounds in the legs, which rarely ever cure.

When he was well enough to speak, we talked to him and asked him some questions about his wife, and the reasons why he killed her, and he then told us what I have related of that resolution, and of his parting, and he besought us we would let him die and was extremely afflicted to think it was possible he might live. He assured us, if we did not dispatch him, he would prove very fatal to a great many. We said all we could to make him live, and gave him new assurances, but he begged we would not think so poorly of him, or of his love to Imoinda, to imagine we could flatter him to life again. But the chirurgeon assured him he could not live, and therefore he need not fear. We were all (but Caesar) afflicted at this news, and the sight was gashly; his discourse was sad and the earthly smell about him so strong that I was persuaded to leave the place for some time (being myself but sickly, and very apt to fall into fits of dangerous illness upon any extraordinary melancholy), the servants and Trefry and the chirurgeons promised all to take what possible care they could of the life of Caesar, and I, taking boat, went with other company to Colonel Martin's, about three days' journey down the river. But I was no sooner gone, but the governor, taking Trefry about some pretended earnest business a day's journey up the river, having communicated his design to one Banister, a wild Irishman, and one of the council, a fellow of absolute barbarity, and fit to execute any villainy, but was rich. He came up to Parham and forcibly took Caesar and had him carried to the same post where he was whipped, and causing him to be tied to it, and a great fire made before him, he told him he should die like a dog, as he was. Caesar replied, this was the first piece of bravery that ever Banister did, and he never spoke sense till he pronounced that word, and if he would keep it, he would declare in the other world that he was the only man, of all the whites, that ever he heard speak truth.

And turning to the men that bound him, he said, "My friends, am I to die, or to be whipped?," and they cried, "Whipped! No, you shall not escape so well." And then he replied, smiling, "A blessing on thee," and assured them, they need not tie him, for he would stand fixed like a rock, and endure death so as should encourage them to die. "But if you whip me," said he, "be sure you tie me fast."

He had learnt to take tobacco, and when he was assured he should die, he desired they would give him a pipe in his mouth ready lighted, which they did, and the executioner came, and first cut off his members, and threw them into the fire; after that, with an ill-favoured knife, they cut his ears, and his nose, and burned them. He still smoked on, as if nothing had touched him. Then they hacked off one of his arms, and still he bore up, and held his pipe; but at the cutting off the other arm, his head sunk and his pipe dropped, and he gave up the ghost without a groan or a reproach. My mother and sister were by him all the while, but not suffered to save him, so rude and wild were the rabble, and so inhumane were the justices, who stood by to see the execution, who after paid dearly enough for their insolence. They cut Caesar in quarters and sent them to several of the chief plantations. One quarter was sent to Colonel Martin, who refused it, and swore he had rather see the quarters of Banister and the governor himself, than those of Caesar, on his plantations, and that he could govern his Negroes without terrifying and grieving them with frightful spectacles of a mangled king.

Thus died this great man; worthy of a better fate, and a more sublime wit than mine to write his praise; yet I hope the reputation of my pen is considerable enough to make his glorious name to survive to all ages, with that of the brave, the beautiful, and the constant Imoinda.

FICTION

FLATLAND: A ROMANCE OF MANY DIMENSIONS, Edwin A. Abbott. (0-486-27263-X)

PRIDE AND PREJUDICE, Jane Austen. (0-486-28473-5)

CIVIL WAR SHORT STORIES AND POEMS, Edited by Bob Blaisdell. (0-486-48226-X)

THE DECAMERON: Selected Tales, Giovanni Boccaccio. Edited by Bob Blaisdell. (0-486-41113-3)

JANE EYRE, Charlotte Brontë. (0-486-42449-9)

WUTHERING HEIGHTS, Emily Brontë. (0-486-29256-8)

THE THIRTY-NINE STEPS, John Buchan. (0-486-28201-5)

ALICE'S ADVENTURES IN WONDERLAND, Lewis Carroll. (0-486-27543-4)

MY ÁNTONIA, Willa Cather. (0-486-28240-6)

THE AWAKENING, Kate Chopin. (0-486-27786-0)

HEART OF DARKNESS, Joseph Conrad. (0-486-26464-5)

LORD JIM, Joseph Conrad. (0-486-40650-4)

THE RED BADGE OF COURAGE, Stephen Crane. (0-486-26465-3)

THE WORLD'S GREATEST SHORT STORIES, Edited by James Daley. (0-486-44716-2)

A CHRISTMAS CAROL, Charles Dickens. (0-486-26865-9)

GREAT EXPECTATIONS, Charles Dickens. (0-486-41586-4)

A TALE OF TWO CITIES, Charles Dickens. (0-486-40651-2)

CRIME AND PUNISHMENT, Fyodor Dostoyevsky. Translated by Constance Garnett. (0-486-41587-2)

THE ADVENTURES OF SHERLOCK HOLMES, Sir Arthur Conan Doyle. (0-486-47491-7)

THE HOUND OF THE BASKERVILLES, Sir Arthur Conan Doyle. (0-486-28214-7)

BLAKE: PROPHET AGAINST EMPIRE, David V. Erdman. (0-486-26719-9)

WHERE ANGELS FEAR TO TREAD, E. M. Forster. (0-486-27791-7)

BEOWULF, Translated by R. K. Gordon. (0-486-27264-8)

THE RETURN OF THE NATIVE, Thomas Hardy. (0-486-43165-7)

THE SCARLET LETTER, Nathaniel Hawthorne. (0-486-28048-9)

SIDDHARTHA, Hermann Hesse. (0-486-40653-9)

THE ODYSSEY, Homer. (0-486-40654-7)

THE TURN OF THE SCREW, Henry James. (0-486-26684-2)

DUBLINERS, James Joyce. (0-486-26870-5)

FICTION

THE METAMORPHOSIS AND OTHER STORIES, Franz Kafka. (0-486-29030-1)

SONS AND LOVERS, D. H. Lawrence. (0-486-42121-X)

THE CALL OF THE WILD, Jack London. (0-486-26472-6)

GREAT AMERICAN SHORT STORIES, Edited by Paul Negri. (0-486-42119-8)

THE GOLD-BUG AND OTHER TALES, Edgar Allan Poe. (0-486-26875-6)

ANTHEM, Ayn Rand. (0-486-49277-X)

FRANKENSTEIN, Mary Shelley. (0-486-28211-2)

THE JUNGLE, Upton Sinclair. (0-486-41923-1)

THREE LIVES, Gertrude Stein. (0-486-28059-4)

THE STRANGE CASE OF DR. JEKYLL AND MR. HYDE, Robert Louis Stevenson. (0-486-26688-5)

DRACULA, Bram Stoker. (0-486-41109-5)

UNCLE TOM'S CABIN, Harriet Beecher Stowe. (0-486-44028-1)

ADVENTURES OF HUCKLEBERRY FINN, Mark Twain. (0-486-28061-6)

THE ADVENTURES OF TOM SAWYER, Mark Twain. (0-486-40077-8)

CANDIDE, Voltaire. Edited by Francois-Marie Arouet. (0-486-26689-3)

THE COUNTRY OF THE BLIND: and Other Science-Fiction Stories, H. G. Wells. Edited by Martin Gardner. (0-486-48289-8)

THE WAR OF THE WORLDS, H. G. Wells. (0-486-29506-0)

ETHAN FROME, Edith Wharton. (0-486-26690-7)

THE PICTURE OF DORIAN GRAY, Oscar Wilde. (0-486-27807-7)

MONDAY OR TUESDAY: Eight Stories, Virginia Woolf. (0-486-29453-6)

NONFICTION

POETICS, Aristotle. (0-486-29577-X)

MEDITATIONS, Marcus Aurelius. (0-486-29823-X)

THE WAY OF PERFECTION, St. Teresa of Avila. Edited and Translated by
E. Allison Peers. (0-486-48451-3)

THE DEVIL'S DICTIONARY, Ambrose Bierce. (0-486-27542-6)

GREAT SPEECHES OF THE 20TH CENTURY, Edited by Bob Blaisdell.
(0-486-47467-4)

THE COMMUNIST MANIFESTO AND OTHER REVOLUTIONARY WRITINGS:
Marx, Marat, Paine, Mao Tse-Tung, Gandhi and Others, Edited by Bob Blaisdell.
(0-486-42465-0)

INFAMOUS SPEECHES: From Robespierre to Osama bin Laden, Edited by Bob
Blaisdell. (0-486-47849-1)

GREAT ENGLISH ESSAYS: From Bacon to Chesterton, Edited by Bob Blaisdell.
(0-486-44082-6)

GREEK AND ROMAN ORATORY, Edited by Bob Blaisdell. (0-486-49622-8)

THE UNITED STATES CONSTITUTION: The Full Text with Supplementary
Materials, Edited and with supplementary materials by Bob Blaisdell.
(0-486-47166-7)

GREAT SPEECHES BY NATIVE AMERICANS, Edited by Bob Blaisdell.
(0-486-41122-2)

GREAT SPEECHES BY AFRICAN AMERICANS: Frederick Douglass, Sojourner
Truth, Dr. Martin Luther King, Jr., Barack Obama, and Others, Edited by
James Daley. (0-486-44761-8)

GREAT SPEECHES BY AMERICAN WOMEN, Edited by James Daley.
(0-486-46141-6)

HISTORY'S GREATEST SPEECHES, Edited by James Daley. (0-486-49739-9)

GREAT INAUGURAL ADDRESSES, Edited by James Daley. (0-486-44577-1)

GREAT SPEECHES ON GAY RIGHTS, Edited by James Daley. (0-486-47512-3)

ON THE ORIGIN OF SPECIES: By Means of Natural Selection, Charles Darwin.
(0-486-45006-6)

NARRATIVE OF THE LIFE OF FREDERICK DOUGLASS, Frederick Douglass.
(0-486-28499-9)

THE SOULS OF BLACK FOLK, W. E. B. Du Bois. (0-486-28041-1)

NATURE AND OTHER ESSAYS, Ralph Waldo Emerson. (0-486-46947-6)

SELF-RELIANCE AND OTHER ESSAYS, Ralph Waldo Emerson. (0-486-27790-9)

THE LIFE OF OLAUDAH EQUIANO, Olaudah Equiano. (0-486-40661-X)

WIT AND WISDOM FROM POOR RICHARD'S ALMANACK, Benjamin Franklin.
(0-486-40891-4)

THE AUTOBIOGRAPHY OF BENJAMIN FRANKLIN, Benjamin Franklin.
(0-486-29073-5)

NONFICTION

PLAYS

THE ORESTEIA TRILOGY: Agamemnon, the Libation-Bearers and the Furies, Aeschylus. (0-486-29242-8)

EVERYMAN, Anonymous. (0-486-28726-2)

THE BIRDS, Aristophanes. (0-486-40886-8)

LYSISTRATA, Aristophanes. (0-486-28225-2)

THE CHERRY ORCHARD, Anton Chekhov. (0-486-26682-6)

THE SEA GULL, Anton Chekhov. (0-486-40656-3)

MEDEA, Euripides. (0-486-27548-5)

FAUST, PART ONE, Johann Wolfgang von Goethe. (0-486-28046-2)

THE INSPECTOR GENERAL, Nikolai Gogol. (0-486-28500-6)

SHE STOOPS TO CONQUER, Oliver Goldsmith. (0-486-26867-5)

GHOSTS, Henrik Ibsen. (0-486-29852-3)

A DOLL'S HOUSE, Henrik Ibsen. (0-486-27062-9)

HEDDA GABLER, Henrik Ibsen. (0-486-26469-6)

DR. FAUSTUS, Christopher Marlowe. (0-486-28208-2)

TARTUFFE, Molière. (0-486-41117-6)

BEYOND THE HORIZON, Eugene O'Neill. (0-486-29085-9)

THE EMPEROR JONES, Eugene O'Neill. (0-486-29268-1)

CYRANO DE BERGERAC, Edmond Rostand. (0-486-41119-2)

MEASURE FOR MEASURE: Unabridged, William Shakespeare. (0-486-40889-2)

FOUR GREAT TRAGEDIES: Hamlet, Macbeth, Othello, and Romeo and Juliet, William Shakespeare. (0-486-44083-4)

THE COMEDY OF ERRORS, William Shakespeare. (0-486-42461-8)

HENRY V, William Shakespeare. (0-486-42887-7)

MUCH ADO ABOUT NOTHING, William Shakespeare. (0-486-28272-4)

FIVE GREAT COMEDIES: Much Ado About Nothing, Twelfth Night, A Midsummer Night's Dream, As You Like It and The Merry Wives of Windsor, William Shakespeare. (0-486-44086-9)

OTHELLO, William Shakespeare. (0-486-29097-2)

AS YOU LIKE IT, William Shakespeare. (0-486-40432-3)

ROMEO AND JULIET, William Shakespeare. (0-486-27557-4)

A MIDSUMMER NIGHT'S DREAM, William Shakespeare. (0-486-27067-X)

THE MERCHANT OF VENICE, William Shakespeare. (0-486-28492-1)

HAMLET, William Shakespeare. (0-486-27278-8)

RICHARD III, William Shakespeare. (0-486-28747-5)